The Reunion at Herb's Café

Books by Dan Jenkins

NOVELS

The Reunion at Herb's Café
Stick a Fork in Me
The Franchise Babe
Slim and None
The Money-Whipped Steer-Job Three-Jack Give-Up Artist
You Gotta Play Hurt
Rude Behavior
Fast Copy
Life Its Ownself
Baja Oklahoma
Limo (with Bud Shrake)
Dead Solid Perfect
Semi-Tough

NONFICTION

Sports Makes You Type Faster
Unplayable Lies
His Ownself: a Semi-Memoir
Jenkins at the Majors
Texas Christian University Football Vault
Fairways and Greens
"You Call It Sports But I Say It's a Jungle Out There"
I'll Tell You One Thing
Bubba Talks
Saturday's America
The Dogged Victims of Inexorable Fate
The Best 18 Golf Holes in America

The Reunion
at Herb's Café

DAN JENKINS

A Novel

Fort Worth, Texas

TCU Box 298300
Fort Worth, Texas 76129
817.257.7822
www.prs.tcu.edu
To order books: 1.800.826.8911

Design by Bill Brammer
www.fusion29.com

Once more for June Jenkins, my dynamite lady,
who was always my Barbara Jane Bookman.

It's the laughter you can carry
Through the years that turn you old.

—from *Baja Oklahoma*
a song by Juanita Hutchins

FOREWORD

Two words.

I promise, just two that will make you laugh and hope for more.

Ready?

Dan Jenkins.

Gotcha.

Dan Jenkins was Texas born, TCU educated, whip smart, and ever ready to see folly when others saw reverence. He was from an early age a print junkie, gobbling up newspaper sports pages, reinventing the form so the absurd and the outlandish had a place at the altar alongside the worshipful.

It's not that he was above his own large soft sweet spot. Mention the Masters Golf Tournament and watch him go all misty describing the bliss of sitting in the clubhouse on Sunday morning with a newspaper, a pot of coffee, and the lineup for the final round.

Dan worked for every print publication except the *Vatican News*. *Sports Illustrated*, *Golf Digest*, the leading Texas newspapers were his primary outlets, but with his first novel, *Semi-Tough*, he moved into the world of books and fictional characters that we knew were hilariously close to the real deal on gridirons and other playing fields.

Semi-Tough, the book and the movie, featured a Texas trio—Billy Clyde Puckett, Marvin "Shake" Tiller, and Barbara Jane Bookman—as the leading characters in the real world of pro football, Texas high rollers, and off-the-field, er, naked calisthenics. It was the first in a lineup of novels that cut through the sanctimonious treatment of big-time sports.

His boldest strike was a fictional "interview" with Tiger Woods in which he cut through the popular deification of Woods and asked about his arrogance around other players, his cheapskate ways with tips, and his cold dismissals of longtime aides.

Woods was not amused, but Dan stood his ground, knowing that the Tiger of TV promotion was not the same man of the clubhouse and player culture.

By the time I met Dan I was prepared to be worshipful, but it was clear he wasn't interested in a fawning fan approach. He always had smart questions about the news. Very quickly Meredith and I became big fans of Dan and his wife, June.

As a longtime big sports-event fawning junkie, from Olympics to Super Bowls and Final Fours, I was thrilled when *Golf Digest* invited me to be a guest writer for a feature called "First Look," an account of a first visit to the Masters.

Best of all, it was a chance to hang with Dan for the weekend on the course and at the evening southern-style dinners organized by the golf writers. They all had tales of the legendary golfers which would be imprudent of me to repeat (but if you spot me in a bar I may be tempted to share one or two). Dan was just one of the boys, his legendary status parked in the spectator's gallery. Here the sweet potato pie had greater standing.

At the end of the weekend Dan looked at me solemnly, shook my hand, and said in his best Bogart style, "We'll always have a Sunday at the Masters," and broke out laughing!

Dan Jenkins always made me laugh and think.

He was Texas large and true as a Masters' green.

In this quintessential Jenkins work, *The Reunion at Herb's Café*, you'll find all of the characters that bring us back to Dan through more than twenty books, fiction and nonfiction.

Puckett the potty mouthed, the laugh-out-loud premise and characters.

Pure Jenkins—the legacy that when I shared the news of this assignment with friends and fellow writers, the reaction was uniform: God, we'll miss him.

Our mutual friend, Bob Schieffer, the CBS legend and another Horned Frog, recalled being on stage with Dan when they were asked what they wanted on their tombstones.

Dan replied that he wanted "I figured it would come to this."

Dan left us laughing and missing him, but *The Reunion at Herb's Café* is a comforting reminder that Dan and all of his character-friends will always be around.

Thank God.

And thank you, Dan.

Tom Brokaw
August 2019

1.

HERB MACKLIN always said he wanted to die in the arms of his dear second wife Nyla, the lady who helped him keep Herb's Café thriving. Even though Nyla saw the place as her chief competition when it came to Herb's attentions. Herb's wish went south the day he decided to clean the gutters on the place himself. Nyla told him only a fool would get up on a ladder at his age, so when Herb fell and died in the arms of a yaupon holly, she found it hard to forgive.

The restaurant had been a landmark forever, and never mind that Herb's Café was not its proper name. The tall sign on the corner of South Side Boulevard and Spurlock Street accurately read:

"Herb Macklin's Restaurant & Bar—Chicken Fried Steaks."

The name had been shortened by faithful regulars like myself.

The building was originally built for Pug's Drive-In. That was during World War II. Carhops wore roller skates to bring mugs of root beer, frozen chocolate malts, chili dogs, and skinny hamburgers to the vehicles. This was obviously before Herb's time, or mine.

A young Herb had seen action in the Korean War after he was drafted into the Army. He bought the restaurant in 1962 when the bar side was a "bottle club." That's when he was married for a short time to "Maureen, the Queen of Mean."

Texans didn't vote in liquor by the drink until 1971. Herb liked to say that if the state had always served mixed drinks, Galveston would have been Las Vegas and San Antonio would have been our New Orleans.

It was my hero and good friend Billy Clyde Puckett who christened Herb's regulars as "Great Americans and wonderful human beings."

Nyla now had a different view of the crowd. She called them "the most pathetic group of no-count, pussy-ruint, hame-heads in God's universe."

I still don't know what a hame-head is. I think it has something to do with a horse. But I felt sure that Nyla included me in the group.

Yeah. Me. Tommy Earl Bruner. As great an American and wonderful human being as you'd ever care to hoist a cocktail with.

* * * * *

IT'S NOT true that I required a sedative when Nyla leased the restaurant to the rainbows. I don't care how people live in private. I've always had friends who were members of the other team. A friend in college was a rainbow, I was certain, although he kept it to himself. He was witty and sharp. An interesting person to sit around and drink coffee with. We talked about stuff other than football. Movies, blues, TV, books that make you laugh. My football teammates made sport of me for befriending him, but he was a better conversationalist than most nose tackles. I've never known what happened to him, or bothered to find out.

I admit I can't take rainbows in groups. When they come

at me in groups they enjoy ridiculing straights with snickering whispers, and prattle on about things I file under Oriental Rugs. Frankly, I don't care for groups of any kind, other than loyal friends and little warm puppies.

The new owners redecorated Herb's to give it the look of a florist shop. They renamed it "Thad and Dorian's Le Pub." That would be Thad Shine, he of the ponytail, and Dorian Wage, he of the pompadour.

The rainbows were rich kids who came from towns named for their relatives. Shine, Arkansas, and Wage, Oklahoma. Thad and Dorian had met at the Culinary Institute of Cuernavaca.

The lads also fancied crewneck sweaters or T-shirts worn under sport coats. That look may have spoken style to the easily led, but to me it looked more like a tourism poster for 1980s Miami. Most shirts I know have collars.

They didn't make it easy on me to befriend, either. What with Thad reminding me that his favorite spectator sport was bodybuilding. And Dorian asking me what a Horned Frog was, and how it differed from, like, a frog?

My educated guess was that Le Pub would not have much staying power when the new owners insisted on closing for dinner after lunch on Sundays and all of Monday.

As long as anyone had known Herb's, it had stayed open seven days a week, every week of the year. I'm saying breakfast, lunch, dinner, after-dinner, and late night. It was open every holiday, including Christmas, Easter, New Year's Eve, and the bowl games on New Year's Day.

The staff liked working holidays. The hefty tips rolled in on holidays. By staff, I refer to the longtime waitresses, Gloria, Agnes, Louise, Bernice, and Mildred, the bartenders from Juanita to Robyn to Trudy to Connie, and the cooks, Will, Opal, and Sugar.

The rainbows made another mistake in adding a selection of adventurous dishes to the menu. I give you the fig and sushi quiche, the rabbit and okra soufflé, the tripe and onions taco, the blended Brussel sprouts, broccoli, cantaloupe, and coconut water smoothie. And in a nod to Texas, the "bullrider's soup." This dazzler came in a bowl of thick brown gunk with what I swear was the brain of a small animal floating on top.

But their biggest mistake was taking the chicken fried steak off the menu and compounding the sin by replacing it with a chicken fried *chateaubriand*, hold the cream gravy.

Which led to eight other regulars and myself putting $100 each in the pot and setting the Over-Under at one year on how long Le Pub would stay in business.

The rainbows were too dumb to realize that Herb's Café had been successful for reasons other than the chicken fried steak. Herb, who consistently wore a suit and tie to work, kept the establishment spotless, the restrooms more so, served a good drink, and everything else to eat was splendid—breakfast at any hour, the fried chicken platter, breaded veal cutlet, stuffed green pepper, bowl of chili, smothered pork chops, chicken and dumplings, corned beef hash, roast beef hash, Irish stew, cheese enchiladas, burgers, the entire menu.

Incidentally, Herb Macklin did not invent the chicken fried steak. That happened on a Texas ranch back in time, and by accident. The same way chili was created by a chuck wagon cook. Herb refined the chicken fried steak and made it the Fort Worth-famous item it has become. He used a thin prime cube steak, tenderized it until it begged for mercy, soaked it in a savory fried chicken batter, cooked it until the batter was slightly crispy, and served it on a slice of white toast or biscuits covered with cream gravy. White gravy, never brown.

When the lads bailed on their three-year lease after ten months, Nyla took their disappearance in stride.

She said, "It's what I should have expected from two simpos who didn't know a biscuit from a donut."

Thad and Dorian's getaway enabled me to scoop the money

pool I'd organized. I won with nine months, twenty-three days.

Nyla received a letter from the lads eventually saying they were sorry they left town hurriedly, but she could expect to start receiving monthly payments from them as soon as they managed to get their Bed & Breakfast up and running in Pugwash, Nova Scotia.

She said, "I'll sit on that till it sings like Tony Bennett."

That's when she made the decision to sell the property to Western City Bank. Let those thieves occupy another corner in town.

Well, I couldn't let that happen. I bought it myself.

2.

I COULD afford to buy the joint by then.

I'd been a hard-working guy who deserved a financial break in my life and it arrived in the form of a wasteland my folks left me. The land only looked suitable for coyotes, wild pigs, deer, and Comanches, but it was discovered to be gurgling with oil and natural gas begging to reach the surface, and this allowed me to wind up richer than an A-rab with six wives and four goats.

My mom and dad, Eileen and Jake, were good-hearted people. They enjoyed great friends, lived a happy life, taught me to laugh at stuff, and raised me to do three things that would be helpful as an adult: read books to improve yourself, do honest work, stay out of jail.

They created a successful furniture store and came to possess the 4,500 acres located forty-five miles west of town from a customer who went broke in the lumber business. He paid them with the land. I took care of the taxes on the property for a number of years, betting on the come, seeing as how I held the mineral rights. The taxes went to a tobacco-chewing county tax assessor-collector who used my ass to give himself a raise every year.

I borrowed the money to pay the taxes from the only banker in town that I knew. He loaned me enough to cover the deal every year after I arranged for Billy Clyde Puckett to send him an autographed football. Billy Clyde's playing days were well behind him, but old running backs don't die, they just wind up with steel plates in their legs.

I'm proud to say my Daddy Jake fought in World War II. He said he used to pray every night that if he survived, the rest of his life would be ice cream. It was years before I found out what he did. He was seventeen and lied about his age to join the Navy the day after Pearl Harbor. I knew he'd served on an aircraft carrier, the USS *Saratoga*, but I was practically grown before I heard any details.

All he ever said as I was growing up was, "The cooks on the *Sara* made good potato soup."

When I'd ask him about the war, my mom would smile and say, "He was kind of a hero, but he doesn't like to talk about it."

He was the gunner in a TBF, a torpedo bomber, which launched off the *Saratoga* when it was part of Admiral "Bull" Halsey's task force in the raid on Rabaul in New Guinea. "I was eighteen years old, for Christ sake," my dad said. "I knew we were in the Pacific Ocean, but I didn't know where."

Daddy Jake's Grumman Avenger sprayed the deckhands and put a hole in an anchored Japanese cruiser before his TBF was shot down. My dad swam a good distance to collect his plane's life raft, and swam a good distance back to rescue his pilot and torpedo officer. He lifted them onto the raft with him. They clung to the raft for three or four hours before they were rescued by the USS *Bailey*, a destroyer.

He said, "We were told there'd be no opposition, but when we were in sight of the Rabaul mainland there were so many Jap planes in the air you'd have thought everybody in that country had learned to fly. Later, after we were deposited on Tulagi in the Solomons, we saw an article in *Stars & Stripes* that said we'd been part of an engagement called 'The Hornets Nest.' Thanks for that lick, Naval Intelligence."

My dad got around to showing me his medals and campaign ribbons one night when I was in high school. They were in his desk at home in a drawer under some business papers. I fondled the Navy Cross, the Distinguished Flying Cross, the Distinguished Service Medal, the Legion of Merit, and a Purple Heart.

I asked him what he did to earn the Purple Heart? All he said was, "I got stung by a jellyfish while I was flopping around in the ocean."

* * * * *

THE IDEA for a reunion occurred to me after I bought Herb's. I wanted to celebrate it in some way. And celebrate the fact that I'd survived my previous adventures in commerce. The only time I showed any smarts was when I turned down one of Foster Barton's get-rich-quick schemes. He invited me to go partners with him on manufacturing and selling school-color caskets.

I said, "Foster, who's gonna buy one besides a Texas Aggie?"

His slump told me he'd rethink the notion.

I sold used Cadillac convertibles until nobody wanted one but Elvis impersonators. But only if it was painted pink. And Elvis impersonators were becoming extinct anyhow.

I went into bulletproof glass and formed Gang Resistant Systems, Inc. This was inspired by the suicide bombers, violent gangs, and vicious teenagers that were multiplying among us, having been raised on blood-thirsty video games, attention-deficit medications, and the skill of inventing cult handshakes.

But I gave up on that quickly. It occurred to me that my product wouldn't do me any good if I were sitting in a Starbucks minding my own business—me and my *Wall Street Journal*—if a lunatic lobbed a bomb into my special breakfast blend.

This was near the end of the nineties, when everybody in Texas was starting to pack a firearm to protect themselves from the guttersnipes. I carry a Glock .19 in a holster on my right hip. I have a clear memory of the first time I was forced to pull it out.

I'd bought a spiral ham in the Overton Park Plaza and was walking to my car when this dude came up to me, flashed a switchblade, and said, "Mister, I believe you got a wad of money in your pocket belongs to me."

I said, "Stay loose, young man. Let me get to my wallet."

I reached back and pulled out the Glock, and said, "Looks like you came up short again, bubba."

His eyes turned into saucers and he took off running, weaving in and out of parked cars. I really can't say whether I'd have shot him or not.

My last venture in those days was when I became a housebuilder. I dipped into the McMansion craze.

You may remember when scores of middle-class Americans overnight decided they needed to live in a McMansion inside a gated community that would keep out other middle-class Americans who might bring in diabetes with them.

Diabetes isn't supposed to be contagious, but if that's a fact I would ask you why every doctor in the United States tells every patient in the United States they have diabetes?

In other news, the problem with McMansions in my experience was that half the people who ordered one couldn't pay for it.

* * * * *

IT WAS a kick to invest money to restore Herb's Café. It deserved to be preserved like Major Ripley Arnold, who founded

Fort Worth for the Frontier Army in 1849.

The major named the fort in honor of General William Jenkins Worth, his commander in the Seminole Wars and Mexican-American War. The big statue of Major Arnold, sword in hand, rises from a bluff behind the Tarrant County courthouse at the north end of downtown.

The major is buried in Pioneer's Rest cemetery on Samuels Avenue, which is not far from where the Army fort was located. Samuels Avenue was the first fine real estate development in Fort Worth. The Victorian homes that were built along the bluff were the city's first "silk stocking" neighborhood.

It came ahead of other desirable sections. Chase Court, south on Hemphill, was the city's first gated community. Pennsylvania Avenue, slightly south of the big Texas and Pacific train station, was once known as "Society Hill." There were other areas developed on the south side. Elizabeth Boulevard was big rich. Park Hill, where Barbara Jane Bookman grew up, was close to big rich. And there was Berkeley Place, where Billy Clyde, Shake, and I grew up. It was comfortable. The west side wasn't developed until the middle twenties and thirties. Why? Because the entire west side was occupied by Camp Bowie, the massive army camp where the Thirty-Sixth Infantry Division trained before our boys in khaki sailed to Europe to win the First World War for Great Britain and France.

Major Arnold had ordered the fort, barracks, mess hall, infirmary, stables, and cemetery built along the bluff for a good reason. It overlooked the Trinity River. The Second Dragoons he commanded could level their muzzle-loading rifles on any Comanches that might be approaching.

"Old Lady" Gilliam in the seventh grade at McLean Junior High taught us that the Comanches were meaner then mountain lions. That among other tidbits.

Reflecting back on it, I think "Old Lady" Gilliam may have been in her twenties then.

3.

BLESS HIS soul, it was Big Ed Bookman, Barbara Jane's daddy, who tracked me down at Herb's to let drop the news that I was soon to take rich.

Bookman Oil & Gas had been making strikes around my coyotes, wild pigs, deer, and Comanches. Big Ed said I owned a payzone waiting to happen, and he was going to become my fifty-fifty partner and dig the goods out of the rocks, dirt, shale, and geology classes for me.

Big Ed said every discovery needed a name. Like Spindletop, the Permian Basin, East Texas, the Spraberry Trend, the Pecos Pool. Mine wasn't nearly as catchy as those, but nevertheless it deserved to be branded. So Big Ed branded my land Comanche Stretch.

He said, "Your property is where the Chief of the Comanches, Quanah Parker, led a band of his braves against Captain Big Foot Wallace and a platoon of Texas Rangers in a war-like contest. It wound up a tie, history allows."

"If you say so," I said.

He said, "Get ready, Tommy Earl. You're gonna be sticking your straw in the ground of Comanche Stretch and sucking up that WhaleAid and Dinosaur Wine for years to come. You're sitting on a deep pool, son."

I said, "Purely out of curiosity, Big Ed, why do I need a partner?"

Big Ed said, "You've never been a roughneck, roustabout, or toolpusher, and you wouldn't know a drilling super if he handed off a football to you. But in case you're dumb enough to go partners with a major right away—your 30 percent to Exxon's 70 percent—I'm here to save your butt."

"I might have been that dumb a minute ago," I said. "Why are you still exploring? You already have more oil than the Sheik of Araby."

He said, "The doctors say I'm healthier than they are. I enjoy a strike. It makes me holler zip-a-dee-do-dah. I'll deal with the majors when the time comes."

I trusted Big Ed. He was the son of a famous wildcatter, "Pecos Pete" Bookman, who started the family fortune that Big Ed carved into an empire.

"Pecos Pete" earned his name by making one of the most famous oil strikes in history. It was in West Texas in 1926, and was given two names—the Pecos Pool and the Yates Field. Yates was the name of the rancher who owned the land. That discovery is still producing.

Big Ed said, "Tommy Earl, you can't have too much whip-out in this world, just for the sake of an emergency."

I said, "I would agree with that even if I didn't have any."

He said, "Whip-out can come in handy when you and me and other folks with common sense are trying to live peaceful lives in the middle of terrorist crazies, suicide nut-cakes, loony-toon anarchists, moron protesters, socialist professors, far-left school teachers, and other misguided sumbitches."

We became partners with a Texas handshake, which is more

binding than a Sicilian mob kiss. The kind you see in the movies where Al Pacino kisses a guy.

When the oil began to lap over my shoes, and the aroma of natural gas started to smell sweeter than a high school date, I was starting to think that Big Ed Bookman was becoming as dear to me as the memories of Jake and Eileen, my dad and mom, who had run out of air to breathe.

I said to my partner, "You're a great man, Big Ed. Wrap me in a robe, put a gold turban on my head, and call me Prince."

✳ ✳ ✳ ✳ ✳

I HAD KNOWN Big Ed in my youth through Billy Clyde and Barbara Jane, but only to say hello and goodbye.

It was when I was building houses and hustled out to West Texas to get in on the McMansion boom that I got to know him well. This was in the one season that Big Ed owned the West Texas Tornadoes in the National Football League, and had hired T. J. Lambert as the head coach and Billy Clyde as the general manager.

Big Ed talked the NFL commissioner, Blinky Bankston, into letting him have an expansion team. If California could have four pro teams, why shouldn't Texas have three?

The commissioner yielded to a finder's fee from Big Ed.

Big Ed placed the team in Gully Creek, Texas, since it was halfway between Lubbock and Amarillo. And semi-historic. Close to where the Spanish explorers stumbled onto the source of the Brazos River, which now meanders a thousand miles through Texas before it dumps itself into the Gulf of Mexico.

Big Ed assumed the Tornadoes would attract fans from the South Plains to the Panhandle. Anywhere that people might hate the Dallas Cowboys or New York City as much as he did. Big Ed didn't care for California either, aside from the Rose

Bowl and Pebble Beach. He liked to say, "Those sillies ain't worth wasting my hatred on 'em."

As for people who live up East, his attitude was well known. He was on record saying, "I'll worry about people in New York City not having enough heat in their homes when I see a drilling platform where the Statue of Liberty used to be."

Fans considered it a miracle when the Tornadoes won the Super Bowl in their one and only season of 1998. I personally thought parity was responsible. No team in the playoffs had posted a better record than 10-6 in the regular season. That Super Bowl was played in Jacksonville, Florida, in a stadium with a corporate name. The Your Money is Our Money Arena.

Coach Lambert's squad was made up of rookies and over-the-hill warriors. His top draft choices were Budget Fowler, a locomotive running back from TCU who had played for T. J., and the blond quarterback-slash-surfer, Shea Luckett, from Southern Cal. Budget had a less-talented brother named Avis who tried football at a small college in Mississippi but quit to play casino poker.

Budget and Shea stood out in the 28-21 victory over the Detroit Lions in the Super Bowl. Budget scored on three long touchdown runs. One was for seventy-six yards on a sweep. The zebra didn't see the clip. Another was his ninety-yard punt return for a touchdown, dancing the last thirty yards. The zebra didn't see the block in the back. Shea Luckett made his own valuable contribution by laying off weed that afternoon.

T. J. was a happy man at the press conference. Billy Clyde took me along. I chose not to wear short pants, sneakers, a golf shirt, and a ballcap so I wouldn't be mistaken for a member of the press.

T. J. reminded everyone that he had earned a Super Bowl ring as a player when he was a defensive stalwart on the New York Giants team of Billy Clyde and Shake Tiller in 1988. Now he'd won a ring as a coach.

T. J. said, "You can call me any time—I pick up after two rings."

He cackled with laughter.

But he momentarily forgot that the era of social-conscience sportswriters was upon us, regrettably.

T. J. said, "I know some of you thought I couldn't keep the wagon between the ditches . . . that I wasn't smart enough to teach the Pledge of Allegiance to a team of fence-climbers."

He was interrupted by moans in the room.

Billy Clyde hung his head and quietly mumbled, "Oh, shit."

Even I could have predicted the explosive headlines we read the next morning in the newspapers. They all added up to:

"Racist Coach Wins Super Bowl."

That morning, T. J. said, "I was making a joke."

Billy Clyde said, "*You* know that. *We* know that. But here lies free speech."

The coach laughed himself into a coughing fit.

* * * * *

DESPITE their success, it was lack of attendance at home games that doomed the Tornadoes. While plans for a ninety-thousand-seat stadium were being drawn up, they played their home games in the county high school stadium that held thirty thousand. Which served the Tornadoes nicely since they never drew more than seven thousand inquisitive souls.

All the while, every high school game, even the one between the Gully Creek Fightin' Roosters and the Salt Fork Hairy-Legged Bats, filled every one of the thirty thousand seats.

Signs popped up on the doors and windows of grocery stores, diners, pool halls, and washaterias. One said: "God's Country Don't Need Pro Football!"

Another one said: "Stop Contaminating Our High School Football."

Big Ed knew West Texas better than I did. I asked him if these people were serious in their dislike of pro football?

He said, "Does a brown bear shit in the Vatican?"

Big Ed liked flashing his Super Bowl ring with the diamonds in it, but he never took financial losses well. That's why he turned the West Texas Tornadoes into the Los Angeles Earthquakes overnight, with the commissioner Blinky Bankston receiving another finder's fee.

He sold the franchise for a tidy profit to a Beijing businessman, a Mr. Wang Yong Kong, who already owned principal stakes in AT&T, United Healthcare, Morgan Stanley, and 256 Szechuan restaurants throughout the United States alone.

We went back to our Fort Worth lives and were enlightened by our experiences.

* * * * *

AFTER MORE strikes were kind to us, and the signs looked promising for others, Big Ed and I were having quail legs and a bowl of chili for lunch one day in his office in the Bookman Oil & Gas Building downtown. We'd begun to have lunch twice a week.

His building was three floors of offices, a map room, board room, dining room, kitchen with chef, gym, library, bar, TV lounge, garage, and a putting green on the roof. He had given me office space on the second floor next to his.

It was in those lunch sessions that I found out there was more to Big Ed's history that I might have guessed. He was born in 1918, nine years prior to the Pecos Pool. His mama's name was Katie. Pete and Katie left the world too soon. They died of heart failure and pneumonia in the thirties. Big Ed inherited the mansion Pete built on Winton Terrace in Park Hill. Barbara Jane grew up in that house, having been born in '65. Her mama was the former Barbara Murphy, now known to everyone as "Big Barb." The Park Hill mansion gave way to Big Ed upgrading the family to the fortress he commissioned in Westover Hills.

The name of Big Ed's high school—and ours—changed while he was in school there. It was Central High in '33 when he entered, and he graduated in '35 after the school was renamed R. L. Paschal High. His daddy sent him off to work in the oil fields for two years before he went to college. "Pecos Pete" said, "Go learn the business. You'll still have plenty of time left to play football and study poetry that don't rhyme."

I knew Big Ed was generous to TCU—there is a science building and a dorm named for him. But I never knew he had lettered at football. As a sophomore he'd been a second-string end on the Orange Bowl team of '41.

After the bowl game, the attack on Pearl Harbor prompted him to join the Army Air Corps, where he hoped to kill Japs and Germans. He yearned to be a fighter pilot, but poor eyesight forced him to teach guys how to march at Drew Field in Tampa for most of the war. He returned to TCU, played two more seasons of football as a second-teamer, and got a degree in geology.

That day at lunch, Big Ed said, "Enjoy your good fortune, Tommy Earl. But don't go buying a fleet of Gulfstreams or collecting a pile of modern art that wouldn't make sense to a plow horse."

I said, "Don't worry. I've seen everything I want to see; I've been everywhere I want to go. I won't even buy a house near you and the other swells. I might lease a share of a jet airplane to get me to TCU's out-of-town games now that Coach 'Puny' Crocker has the Frogs winning again."

Big Ed said, "You're entitled to some toys."

I said, "But I have to tell you, Big Ed. If you see me with a fleet of Gulfstreams, it'll be after I've bought a submarine."

4.

THE CAST of regulars who gathered in the bar at Herb's increased to become a varied assortment of citizens. I would have said they were an *eclectic* crowd, but I hate that word with every fiber in my body.

People who use the word eclectic think it makes them sound smart, but I say it only makes them sound silly, in an eclectic sort of way.

The well-established among the regulars starts off with Loyce Evetts, the wealthy ne'er-do-well who kept bimbos on the side.

Foster Barton was prominent. He owned and ran "a funeral home for dead people," he called it.

There was Dr. Neil Forcheimer, the TCU professor of political science and world history, discounting Egypt's fraudulent claims. He believed everything was a moral question, apart from football.

Hank Rainey was in there. The society carpenter. He had bedded down more well-off housewives than a tennis pro.

Doris and Lee Steadman were steady customers in their earlier years. That was when Doris collected lovers like women collect shoes. But her pace had slowed appreciably. Lee, who was still selling carpet, had remained capable of suggesting the best route to take if you were driving somewhere in town. That's if you had a lifetime to listen.

Shorty Eckwood was a stump of a little gray-haired man who could have been anywhere from 90 to 105 years old. He was a retired railroad worker who dropped into Herb's twice a day for a beer and a free meal of Premium crackers with ketchup and Tabasco. His calling in life was to remind people that the town had sports heroes before Sam Baugh and Davey O'Brien in football and Ben Hogan and Byron Nelson in golf.

They were the Fort Worth Panthers who won the Texas League and Dixie Series six times in the twenties. Shorty's daddy said his son was busy getting born and missed seeing that bunch play. A lineup that included Ziggy Sears, Cecil Combs, Possum Moore, Jack and Clarence "Big Boy" Kraft, with Joe Pate, Paul Wachtel, and Lil Stoner on the mound.

But Shorty had his own heroes, the '37 and '39 Fort Worth Cats who also won the Texas League and Dixie Series. Ask him anything about their immortal infield of Lee Stebbins, Rabbit McDowell, Buster Chatham, and Frank Metha, or how the outfield changed from Homer Peel, Hugh Shelley, and Freddie Frink to Carl Kott, Walt Cazen, and Johnny Stoneham. Both clubs relied on the same two pitching aces, Ed ("Bear Tracks") Greer and Jackie Reid.

Shorty would say, "Boy, hidy—that was baseball. The studs stayed here in the off season. They sold tires and used cars and men's clothing and met their wives here. I wouldn't trade one pot of collards for the whole major league."

Among the new drop-ins was Hoyt Newkirk. He moved here from Ruidoso after losing his job as the manager of the Mescalero Country Club & Casino Resort. The Apaches found out he wasn't part Indian. Hoyt did look more like a pot-bellied fiddle player than Geronimo.

"Leaving Ruidoso was a good thing," Hoyt said. "I couldn't beat them four-legged athletes. I couldn't do it no more than I could beat them Apaches at keeping up with their money." Hoyt settled here and was looking around for "opportunities."

Chester Wooten managed Wooten's Drugstore three blocks away but he could usually be seen in Herb's doctoring his sorrow over the Texas Rangers throwing away the World Series in 2011 to the St. Louis Cardinals. I tried to soothe him by reminding him it was only baseball.

Donny Chance, a portrait painter, provided a test for Will Vinson and the other cooks by inventing his own dinners. His latest was the Bodobber. A hamburger pattie smothered in cheese, crispy-chewy bacon, chopped onions, chopped green peppers, and scrambled eggs poured over all of it. Hard to look at it.

Jeff Sagely was a nighttime regular. In the daytime he operated his own food wagon in Trinity Park. Cyclists and joggers stood in line for his spicy hotdogs and tacos. He made a living despite the fact that he was robbed once a week at gunpoint.

Three punks in their twenties were in and out of Herb's often enough.

Bobby Downs, who had brought back the ducktail haircut, had spent most of his time ingratiating himself to Herb Macklin as the son Herb never had. That's when Herb was still of this world.

Bobby's running mates were Clarence "Dorito" Bracy and "Everywhere Red" Fuqua. The three of them were bagmen for bookmakers operating out of hotel suites downtown. I knew the bookies well—Randy "Boots" Dunlap, Max "Montana Slim" Kramer, and Alvin "Circus Face" Jordan.

Bobby worked for Montana Slim. Dorito worked for Boots, a rodeo cowboy in his youth. Dorito got his nickname by way of his favorite entrée—a can of bean dip with Doritos. Red Fuqua worked for Circus Face, a pudgy fellow with a fixed smile who answered his phone the same way every time. He'd say, "Tell me."

Two other new regulars were the Low-Flying Ducks, as Foster Barton named them. They were women in their rapidly advancing sixties.

One was Gladys Hobbs, a humorless person who owed a dress shop down the street, drank straight-up gin martinis, and lived alone but within carry-home distance of the restaurant.

Her position on current events, wars, politics, sports, religion, or anything else was: "I couldn't care less."

The other one was Cora Abernathy. She never shut up, but never said anything interesting. That was unless you cared to hear that the first car she owned was a Plymouth Barracuda, or listen to the list of items she purchased at Costco the other day.

Cora, who was part owner of the Hasty Bakery, was of interest to most of us because her three husbands all drowned accidentally in their bathtubs at home. But no one had been able to muster up enough stamina to ask Cora for the details.

Cora did confess that she'd tried to interest *The Guinness Book of World Records* in the oddity, but she never heard back from them.

"Some people," she said.

In case you didn't know what a Low-Flying Duck was, Foster Barton was eager to define it for you. It was a lady into her sunset years who wouldn't resist a charitable romp.

5.

IF YOU were scoring, you were aware that I was twice divorced by the time I made my contribution to America's energy independence. First I split from Sheila Baker, mother of our two kids, and then from Tracy Hopkins, the shapely adorable who took me hostage when she was a lingerie model.

If I'd been married to Sheila when the oil and gas bubbled up, huge sums of my cash would have disappeared quicker than I could say Neiman Marcus.

Upper class parents, Country Day private school. Sheila was raised a good little spender. At a certain point, you could find more fashionable frocks in Sheila's possession than you would in the closets of a dictator's wife.

Minor historical note. I followed Billy Clyde, Barbara Jane, and Shake Tiller by two years at Paschal High and TCU. But I was never in Billy Clyde's class as a running back. Not many were.

Tampa Bay drafted me in the ninth round but all I did was watch film and manage three or four carries in the fourth quarter of games the Bucs had already lost in lifeless fashion. Tampa Coach "Punchy" Hayes was a nice fellow, but he'd have been more successful, if you asked me, as a dog whisperer.

I wasn't equipped with the size and speed to hack it in the NFL anyhow. It was why I lost interest in the game after two seasons and joined the ranks of great Americans and wonderful human beings.

It did amuse Herb Macklin to spread it around that I'd made All-Nonchalant three straight seasons when I played for TCU.

Herb wasn't always that hilarious.

Sheila and I met in college our junior year and fell into something similar to love. She was cute. She had mastered the trick of laughing at the right things. This was before we were married and she became serious about every damn thing in the entire world.

We married soon after graduation. That was what you did in those days if you wanted to be accepted as a grown-up.

Sheila's parents, Rob and Fiona, sent us on a trip to Europe for our honeymoon. I agreed to it after they let me pick the countries. We dropped in on England, Scotland, Ireland, France, Germany, Italy, Switzerland, and Spain. Skipped the ones I thought would be boring—Poland, Belgium, Holland, all the Bulgarias. I was too stupid then to know that Prague was the prettiest city any invader had ever thrown a blitzkrieg at.

I gladly give Sheila credit for forcing us to go there for a day. I enjoyed the beauty of the city. She enjoyed the boutiques she had read about.

Sheila's folks had suggested we sail over and back on a luxury liner, as they once had. Sheila thought it sounded romantic. So did I—until I thought about the icebergs, and the deal about women and children first in the lifeboats, and wondering if there'd be enough lifeboats to go around, and weighing the horrors of drowning against the horrors of being stranded in a lifeboat with screeching kids.

It was a win when I talked Sheila into going American.

Fortunately this was back when air travel was a pleasant experience. First class was plush, cocktails and food came swiftly, the movie didn't have a monster or a robot in it, and the flight attendants were attractive and energetic. None of them looked as tired as Aunt Irene when they shuffled up and down the aisle.

In other words, air travel was nothing like today. Every terminal you're trapped in now is a holding pen for vagrants, and every trip on a commercial airliner is a flying pigsty.

The short version of our honeymoon is that Sheila visited every cathedral and museum in every country while I comparative-taste-tested every sidewalk café in every country.

Not that she didn't do a little shopping. Her mother had slipped her a charge card, and said, "If you see anything interesting, buy me one too." That was all the encouragement she needed to buy two scarves for a total of $1,900.

I judged Switzerland was easily the tallest country we saw. Italy was the oldest. It was a surprise to discover that the Germans, French, and Italians spoke better English than the Scots and Irish. The food was excellent everywhere but in Spain. That's where I found too many things on my plate that weren't completely dead yet.

We returned to settle into the life of a typical American married couple. We fought about money and everything else.

Where to go to dinner, what to order for dinner, what movie to see, what TV channel to watch, what books to read, what people she liked that I couldn't stand, what people I liked that she couldn't stand. And politics, of course—she the limousine liberal who felt bad for the "little people," and me the jolly independent who tended to vote against most incumbents.

Rob and Fiona helped us buy a modest house on Stadium Drive not far from the TCU campus. They helped support us in the early going. Rob was a partner in the law firm of Baker, Anderson, Minter, Morris, O'Malley & Florsheim. I may not need to mention that Rob was a two from the tips at Shady Oaks and River Crest.

While I struggled in business ventures, Sheila made her parents proud by clawing her way into the Junior League.

Our kids were born one year apart, our son first. Sheila named him Bryson. I named him Tommy Earl Junior. It was easier to remember. A year later when our daughter entered the world, I suggested something simple. Janie, Sally, Sarah. But I was outvoted by her mother.

Sheila had discovered the name Aubyn in an art book. One of those things that covers a coffee table. She spelled it for me.

"Aubyn?" I said with a look that failed the happy test.

She said, "It's perfect. It will help her be rushed by the best sororities when the time comes. I know this by experience." Sheila was a Chi Omega who'd never completely recovered from it.

She was already working on her long-range goal in life. Which was to see her daughter taken into the Junior League the same year that she, the mom, was elected president of the Junior League.

Some women want love.

"*Aubyn?*" I said again.

"Yes," she said defiantly.

I said, "Darn it, I missed an opportunity. If I'd known we were gonna have a daughter called Aubyn, I'd have named our son Climpson."

I watched our kids scream, kick, cry, squirm, and poke Snickers bars in their birthday cakes until the fifth grade in elementary school—when they thought they'd become adults. I endured them learning to speak fluent smart-ass in junior high. I tolerated them not speaking to me at all through three years of high school.

Sheila allowed it. She said she didn't want "the munchkins" growing up to think they weren't as good as everybody else. Her use of the word "munchkins" by itself started me thinking it might be time to hit the silk.

With blood, sweat, and bank loans I came up with the tuition, spending money, and cars they needed while they were at TCU and living on campus. Sheila insisted they live among other students to enjoy "campus life." I said they did it to get away from the noise at home.

I don't know how our kids were accepted by any university in these United States. They weren't from the Congo, Mozambique, India, Pakistan, Iran, Syria, Malaysia, or any of those neat countries in South America.

It was a welcome savings when Tommy Earl Junior was given a full football scholarship at TCU. He started at safety his last two seasons. He was on the team that went to a bowl in Houston that I think was called the Houston Bowl.

He was an excellent student and graduated with a business degree and landed a job with a sports management company in Dallas. He's become a VP and lists two Mavs, three Rangers, and three Cowboys among his clients.

Aubyn was swept into Chi Omega without a bump in the road. She graduated with a degree in art history. I made the mistake of commenting that her degree would be useful someday if she decided to live in Italy.

It was meant as a joke. Aubyn laughed. But Sheila greeted it with a look of scorn.

When Aubyn isn't absorbed in a volunteer project, or striving to become a member of a committee that was raising money for the Kimbell Museum, the symphony, or the local film festival, she dates—hooks up, rather. She's husband-shopping but holding out for a Wall Street type, even if he wears bow ties and likes to sip a mocha chocko mooka cuckoo latte.

She brings most of her dates around to meet me. The one I remember best was short and I heard him utter only one sentence. Which was, "I have to take this." And he took his smartphone into another room and stayed a half hour.

Sheila and I were on our way to a divorce by the time the kids entered college. She said I had changed. I said she had changed. She said I changed more.

She accused me of never having recovered from my football days, even if I was never more than everyday, ordinary as a player, and it was all she could do to pretend I was more than that. Then I dragged her off to Tampa, Florida, which wasn't her idea of paradise.

"Mine either," I said. "What did you hate the most about it? The humidity or the bugs?"

"You," she said.

"Old everyday, ordinary me," I said. "You know, Sheila, it's good to know what you've really thought of me all these years. I should have received some kind of an Idiot of the Year Award for marrying you in the first place."

One of our last battles was the day she launched into an exhaustive rage over I can't remember what. I do know it was severe enough for her to donate all my high school and college letter jackets to the Union Gospel Mission.

Our squabbles kept piling up until a day when I decided to gather up the stuff I wanted and bail out. Leave our fun-filled chit-chats behind for good. I moved into an old department store downtown that had been transformed into a luxury apartment building.

My last words to her were, "All the best, Sheila. I hope you find the Kappa Sig pledge captain you should have married in the first place. If you can't find one by yourself, I'm sure Rob and Fiona will buy you one."

I believe she told me there was something I could do to myself.

6.

WHILE I WAS wallowing in the single life I let Loyce Evetts drag me with him on a search to upgrade his mistresses. I found myself browsing through parlors named Tricky Chicks, Francine's Flimsies, and Naughty Girls Lingerie. It was scenic.

I can assure you I would never have gone near those parlors on my own. Not unless I was disguised as a colonel in the French Foreign Legion and dressed for parade.

Loyce claimed that the shelf life of a mistress was eighteen months, depending on a man's threshold for boredom. It was drawing close to the moment to replace Heather and Amber, the current bimbos he was keeping stashed in expensive apartments on the west side of town.

Loyce could afford high-rent mistresses. He was from old wealth that was derived from oil, ranching, grain, real estate, and stock portfolios. His family had done very well in North Texas near the Oklahoma border. Up there where the wind is the same color as the Red River.

He had a wife, Pamela, but he detested her. Primary among his reasons was that she had become a workout freak and exercised herself down to a skeleton. For that, she gave up tennis, golf, bridge, and eating.

Pamela did keep shopping on her activity list. Her best friends were now the sales ladies in the upscale stores and boutiques in the DFW "Metroplex," as some genius named it. And burgeoning Dallas alone was beginning to seize parts of Oklahoma and Kansas as suburbs.

Loyce put a nagging question to me:

"Is it asking too much of a man to want a wife who likes to eat normal food instead of roots, and drink something besides bottled cucumber water?"

Loyce and Pamela rarely spoke. His idea of a conversation was, "Shall we dine at the club this evening? This could be Seaweed Night."

Loyce tried to drive Pamela to a divorce by giving her presents on her birthday, Christmas, and their anniversary that plugged into the wall. His mistresses received the big rocks.

He was hoping Pamela would ditch him for the male skeleton she met while training for the city's annual traffic-clog, otherwise known as the Fort Worth Marathon. He said, "They can chew pumpkin seeds together."

He added, "One valuable lesson I've learned, Tommy Earl. If it flies, floats, or fucks, lease it."

* * * * *

WHEN I was introduced to Tracy Hopkins at Naughty's that afternoon, she wasted no time using her salesmanship skills on me. By that I mean she launched directly into sexual harassment.

It wasn't as if I'd never been sexually harassed before. I was sexually harassed by babes all through high school and college.

It was unavoidable if you shaved and showered every day, wore clean clothes, owned a car, and played in the backfield.

Things are different these days. The Wasted Guitar Player Look is still around, I've noticed. Certain women find themselves attracted to guys in soiled jeans and grimy work shirts who go through life with the quizzical look of someone who has smoked a pound of weed every day since the ninth grade.

He's a guy with a head of sixties hair. A guy whose best guess as to what country America won its independence from was . . . *Portugal?*

The Caveman Look provides competition. Here you find babes who go for guys with facial hair you'd normally see on a Schnauzer. This is a guy who thinks it makes him pass for worldly if he can stroke his beard and quote something Bruce Springsteen said.

Tracy Hopkins led me into a private dressing room where she modeled two scanty items she thought would interest "the lady in my life." What interested me most was Tracy. She was hot. Ferociously hot. I mean hot like don't touch her anywhere, you'll scald your hand.

Tracy slid in next to me on a sofa in a private room and although I remained clothed, she toyed around with my body parts while suggesting things we could do in bed together if we were a couple. Most of the suggestions sounded familiar, but there were others I didn't think were physically possible. Not that I let that stand in the way of wedlock, however.

We were married the first time in the University Christian Church by a pastor and geology professor at TCU who'd been a friend of the football program. He handed out passing grades to the gridsters in a course called Human Activity. I heard it was patterned after a course that was available throughout the Southeastern Conference.

A couple of months later one of Tracy's girlfriends said our marriage wasn't legit. "Christian" didn't sound like a real religion to her. We should find a Baptist or a Methodist to do it right.

I said, "Tracy, University Christian is the Disciples of Christ. It's the church I was raised in."

She said, "Tommy Earl, every religious person is a disciple of Christ. I know I am, when I have the time."

We were married again on an afternoon in an old two-story house converted into a Baptist church on Jennings Avenue on the south side. The minister introduced himself as Reverend Horace "Corky" Matthews. Tracy's mother, Velma, the Single Mom from Hell, stood up with her. T. J. Lambert, who was coaching the Horned Frogs' football fortunes then, was my best man.

When the minister stretched out the ceremony with talk about partnership, sharing, forgiveness, and understanding, T. J. butted in.

"Corky, old buddy," T. J. said, "you want to shift into your hurry-up offense? I didn't come here to piss away the whole afternoon."

Dr. Horace "Corky" Matthews hastily declared us man and wife. I tipped him a hundred, and T. J. gave him another hundred, and we were out of there.

I couldn't spare the time for a honeymoon. I was still in the McMansion business and forced to keep tabs on the crews who worked for me. It was where I learned never to let an employee order materials for you. He'll double what you need. Half will be for him—and the business he'll start up.

* * * * *

TRACY HAD been living with her single mom in a condo in a neighborhood in West Arlington. The town of Arlington had existed for years as nothing more than a stop for gas or a liquor store if you were driving the thirty miles from Fort Worth to Dallas. But now Arlington is where the footballing Dallas Cowboys and baseballing Texas Rangers perform in modern stadiums, and Arlington is now bigger than Pittsburgh.

Tracy had described her mother as a "smart business woman," although Velma had never held down a job.

That's not altogether accurate. Velma worked harder to trick the system than she would if she labored nine to five doing chores for somebody else. It had to take considerable energy or creativity or both for her to earn $40,000 a year by collecting social security checks—most of them for dead people, and receiving payments for her non-existent disability, claiming food stamps to sell to others, receiving child support for her non-existent triplets, and from staying glued to the welfare rolls.

But you had to say Velma gave her daughter a well-rounded education. She hammered into Tracy never to let herself become involved with a man who didn't have a steady job, a car that started, and a roof over his head.

Velma convinced Tracy that her pretty face and killer body were going to do more for her in life than going to school to learn how many state capitals she could name.

Tracy resigned from Naughty's and moved into my department-store apartment to play the role of housewife, which didn't include cooking, I discovered. No problem. We were within a short walk to a dozen restaurants that featured foods of the world. Many of those eateries wouldn't stay in business for longer than six months, but they'd be replaced by others.

I had chosen an apartment on the second floor in case of fire. Easier to escape. Always take an edge when possible, I say.

The real estate agent tried to interest me in a pad on the tenth floor where I would have a panoramic view of the city. I explained to him that I was born and raised here and was more than familiar with the skyline.

My folks loved Fort Worth. They talked about what I'd missed in their day. Leonard Brothers Department Store, for one thing. It was an enormous three-story building covering an entire city block downtown where people could buy everything from a loaf of bread to a toy wagon to a tractor. People came from miles around to shop there at bargain prices, and they did it for more than sixty years.

The malls killed every department store in their path. That was before the malls themselves began to lose their appeal, except in the parking lots, which was where you went if you were overcome with a yearning to get car-jacked.

My folks loved the ornate movie houses that stretched along Seventh Street in the heart of downtown—the Hollywood, Worth, and Palace. When my dad came home after the war, he and my mom looked forward to seeing live entertainers like the Mills Brothers, the Ink Spots, and the Andrews Sisters, who would appear live on stage before the movie. TV had yet to exist, as you might guess.

Since Tracy no longer worked, she constantly invited friends over for drinks who stayed far too long. They were girlfriends from Naughty's, Tricky's, and Flimsies. They would drink too much wine, and confine the conversation to the manly equipment they'd known on an intimate basis recently.

"Sex drives men crazy," a model said one night. That lured me into the discussion.

"Sports drives men crazier than sex," I said. "There's proof of this if you watch football on TV. When has sex ever encouraged a man to strip down to his jock and paint his entire body crimson and white?

"Better still, have any of you known sex to make a man sit outdoors in a stadium during a snowstorm with the letters 'L.S.U.' painted in purple and gold on his bare chest?"

A girl said, "I've never tried acid."

I laughed but she didn't know why. Then I said, "I'm sure none of you have gone to dinner with a man who wore a block of cheese on his head, right?"

The girls stared at each other in disbelief.

In the year and a half of our marriage I did my best to smooth out Tracy's rough edges. I tried to interest her in reading the newspaper to become more conversant with current events. She tried but not for long. She came across too many "French words" she didn't get.

"For example?" I asked.

She pointed out three examples. Naive, despair, colony.

I tried her on a book, a murder mystery with "Prey" in the title, which may have thrown her off. She tossed it after eight pages, complaining that nobody had been killed yet.

Tracy wasn't careful in her manner of speech. One evening I suggested she might consider in moments of anger to use expressions such as, "Lord have Mercy," or, "Land o' Goshen," instead of, well, just to cite one example, referring to someone as a "a limp-dick shit-face."

"What's wrong with that?" she said.

Eventually I discovered that I'd married the only woman in America who had never seen *Casablanca*.

She went the distance with the movie, but found it too complicated to keep up with, and on top of everything else, it was "really stupid."

Her review:

"A chick who looks like Ilsa would never run off with a skinny guy from Checkosloggia. *Are you kidding me*? You can bet your ass she'd hang with Rick. The foreign dude don't even have a job. But on a rainy night she goes off with him in a rickety old airplane. It's no even a jet, for God's sake."

* * * * *

I HAVE to confess I was more than slightly relieved the night Tracy said, "Honey Pie, I don't want to hurt your feelings, but I've given a lot of thought to it and I don't think I'm suited for this marriage gig."

She told me a girlfriend who had worked at Naughty's had been in touch with her and said she should come to Shreveport—it was a gold mine for cocktail waitresses in the casinos.

We parted friends. She moved to Shreveport but her mother didn't go along. In Velma's business world it would have required filling out too many forms and possibly running into unforeseen roadblocks that would be created by what she called "those good-for-nothing jokers in the Federal gubmint."

The first time I heard from Tracy was after the news reached her that I had "fallen in an oil well." She badly needed a new car and it looked like I was in a position to buy her one. I sent her the money and was informed that the amount wasn't enough for a Mercedes. I apologized and sent her the balance.

The last letter from her said:

"Hi, Tommy Earl. Life is good here. Did you know the Red River runs through downtown Shreveport like it does between Oklahoma and Texas. That astounds me. Like how did it get to Louisiana, you know? There is a reason you haven't heard from me. I have been busy moving up in the world. I'll have you know I've risen from a cocktail waitress to a blackjack dealer!

"The school for dealers is long and hard, but I made it through. Now I have a profession I can take pride in.

"I hope you are doing good, but how could you not be? Mama taught me a long time ago never to feel sorry for anybody who makes more money than I do.

"Hit 11, stay on 12.

"Love, Tracy."

7.

IN THE marriage game, you could compare me to the stubborn football coach who keeps the short-side option in his offense. He buys into a wizard's arithmetic that assures him the play works more often than it doesn't. But it never has, never does. I, on the other hand, am now proud to offer evidence that if a man falls in love enough times, he'll finally get it right.

My personal life changed from mystery and guesswork to love and laughter when I connected with Olivia Ann Randall. Olivia was the best thing the millennium brought into my life. Or back into my life.

We dated our first two years at TCU. That was in the pre-Sheila era. For a spell Olivia and I fell into deep like. She was a stunner, a local lass. She was a year behind me in high school and college, but we knew each other fairly well.

Even though she wasn't from a rich family she was scooped up by the Pi Phis at TCU. I'm happy to report she survived the experience. I was recruited by the frats but I passed. I wanted to pick my own pals.

Olivia became a better friend in college. My other pals were my teammates. The close-friend thing with Olivia continued after we were out of school, but the deep-like thing ran into trouble. Our attitudes differed on the value of a degree. I graduated, but I didn't need a piece of parchment to tell me I was smarter than any white guy who wore his baseball cap backwards.

College for me was football and hanging out. Olivia majored in journalism, specifically communications, and worked hard to acquire an education that would help her carve out a career in TV.

Career?

Wasn't a career something that happened down the road? Some guy offered you a job, you took it and worked hard enough at it to deserve an office with a window?

I never counted on taking rich, but I don't apologize for it, either.

Olivia Ann is a brunette who wears her hair at shoulder length most of the time, but she will yield to fashion trends. She's as statuesque and beautiful as ever. Living proof that forty is the new thirty.

We would run into each other in town. Have lunch. She had gone from college to an entry-level job at KVAT, one of the local TV stations. But she was brighter than everybody there, and it didn't take many years for her to became the station manager. She's still the boss, good at it—irreplaceable, in fact. She loves her work, her profession.

Like me, she had survived two marital train wrecks. Both were the result of choosing looks over character. Neither marriage lasted long. It was fortunate no kids were involved.

Her first train wreck was with Lance Early, the station's prime-time news anchor. He was upbeat, ever smiling. That was at work and when they went to lunch or dinner together.

It slowly dawned on Olivia that they only dined in restaurants where a framed photo of Lance hung on the wall. Sometimes you had to look closely to find it among the Cowboys, Rangers, Mavericks, stock car drivers, local jazz musicians, and community theater performers.

This confined their dining pleasures to Ted's Turkey & Dressing, Wanda's Casseroles, The Burger You Remember, Rodeo Riley's Leather-Slappin' Buckaroo Steaks, Nell's Ham Bits & Navies, and Zapata's Nuclear Tacos.

Lance was boycotting Lucy's Catfish Festival. His photo had accidentally been knocked off the wall, breaking the glass and frame. Lucy expected Lance to pay for having it fixed. Their argument was ongoing. It was a matter of pride to someone of Lance's stature.

Lance had two things in common with the majority of local news anchors across the width and breadth of America. He was handsome, and he was stupid. If somebody didn't write it for him, he couldn't say it or think it.

Olivia was the producer of the prime-time news when they married, and his producer eleven months later, after they divorced. One of them had to go. Particularly after Lance kept hounding the station manager, Vic Bishop, to let him interview guests on the program. Like professors and politicians. They would discuss the Middle East and other problems of the world.

Lance argued, "As a news anchor, I should discuss big topics."

Olivia sat in on the meeting the day Vic Bishop said to the news anchor, "Lance, you are a likable presenter, but you know nothing about the Middle East and the Israeli-Palestinian conflict. You are *local*, you are not *network*. I don't want to hear any more about this."

Lance said, "I know everything I need to know about the Jews and Palestinians. They're the same people. So . . . you know . . . like . . . get over it, guys."

She and Vic exchanged looks. Later that day she was instructed by Vic Bishop to "find that moron a job somewhere as far away from me as possible."

She touched base with a Hollywood guy she'd met at a convention who was looking for someone to host a daytime game show he was producing for a network. All he said about the show was that it involved real married couples throwing food at each other.

Olivia sold the producer on Lance, saying women will love his checkered suits, and that Lance and cue cards would become a romance to rival Lancelot and Guinevere.

Her second train wreck was Gary Shelton, the investment counselor. He was handsome and smooth. Smooth enough to make one client rich and happy so he could attract others.

Their marriage lasted less than two years—Gary disappeared one day and has yet to be found. There had been no news regarding him in six years. Istanbul, is Olivia's best guess.

Gary often spoke of Istanbul and other cities in Turkey. He could be dead by now, or a Turk.

It took her a year to obtain a "missing spouse" divorce. It wasn't so much the eternal waiting she found annoying as it was having to convince a series of judges that Gary Shelton was, as a matter of fact, missing.

She confessed to me, "Gary's self-worship should have been apparent when we moved into the house across from Colonial Country Club. Gary took the largest closets for himself. He devoted as much time to color-coordinating his wardrobe as he did stealing everybody's life savings."

Olivia and I reconnected when we were dealing with the single life, even though she was devoted to her job and I was busy keeping up with my money. Trying to put it somewhere safe from the thieves chewing on my pants leg.

We resumed our lunches and threw in a dinner when she could tear herself away from the TV station.

There was always a tornado alert.

8.

I SHAN'T soon forget the day we met for lunch at the Fort Worth Club downtown. It was a slow news day, so we strung out the lunch for two hours. Olivia introduced me to an eighteen-dollar bottle of Napa red that she insisted was as good as a phony two-hundred-dollar bottle from somewhere you never heard of and can't pronounce.

The lunch ended on a level of the club's parking garage surprisingly—and spontaneously—in hungry hugs and a series of juicy kisses. Certainly one of those moments that made me wonder about this and that and other activities.

From there on we did dinner dates and flowers, and staying up all hours. Sleepovers found their way into our lives. It's where I discovered that love made the sleepover more satisfying than your basic athletic event.

We introduced our doggies to each other. Mine was a half-breed debutante that chose me at a rescue shelter. Her gaze melted me. I named her Dixie.

Olivia's doggie was a three-thousand-dollar Maltese she named Virginia Katherine after Fort Worth's Ginger Rogers, whose real name was Virginia Katherine McMath.

The dogs bonded like sorority sisters, or like sorority sisters would if some of their parents weren't better off financially than others.

Being in love makes a man do goofy things. Go to the zoo. Go to ball games. Go to Bass Hall to see a road company screw up a Broadway musical classic. Go see a foreign film. Suddenly prefer Chicken Kiev by candlelight over cheese enchiladas. Or—and I never thought I'd say this—prefer fusilli with a light tomato sauce by candlelight over spaghetti and meat sauce.

Marriage came creeping into my thoughts quicker than I might have suspected. But I was a pushover after too many years on the dreaded hit-and-miss single circuit. It happened that Olivia was thinking the same thing.

One evening I said, "How do you feel about two people joining up in matrimony if it doesn't take too much of their time?"

She said, "You mean if two people were to marry because they were in love with each other, not somebody else?"

"That would be part of the plan."

"I'm a two-time loser, don't forget."

"I knew we had more than one thing in common."

"But you have an excuse."

"I do?"

"You didn't know any better."

"True enough. I was an idiot."

"You're not an idiot now. You're rich."

"Yeah, by accident."

"You are not an idiot, Tommy Earl. I'm not capable of marrying a third idiot."

I said, "Would you insist on a honeymoon?"

She shook her head. "Too busy."

I said, "What about a wild weekend of sex and room service at the Omni Hotel?"

"That, I could work in."

Before we did the vow thing, we mutually decided to make a fresh start on our living quarters.

I rented my downtown apartment. I paid off the mortgage on her Colonial house and sold it for a healthy profit in her behalf. She picked out an unpretentious house that I bought for us in the River Crest neighborhood. It came with a lawn and trees, front and back. The doggie people were pleased.

We were married by a justice of the peace at the courthouse and went to Herb's Café for dinner. Olivia reminded me that I'd taken her to dinner at Herb's on our first date when we were in college.

Loyce Evetts pulled out his money clip and said to Olivia, "Peaches, what's it gonna take for me to money-whip you away from this slug?"

She turned to me with a smile.

"You didn't tell me Loyce went to Baylor."

Loyce said, "Damn, I miss the days when hundred dollar bills made pretty ladies horny."

* * * * *

LOOKING BACK on it, I have to say I owe a debt to Tracy Hopkins. If it hadn't been for Tracy, I might never have learned to trade in hot—and smokin' hot—for classy and good-natured.

9.

I LOOKED after the re-do of Herb's Café without kicking a small child, or cussing another moron trying to kill people in his Big Dooley truck. A blissful marriage does this to a person. Olivia liked watching me bring the place back to what it resembled before the rainbows turned it into the Nightmare Pub on Swamp Fiend Street, not to suggest a movie title.

I found a wallpaper close to the caricatures of poodle dogs that once covered the dining room walls. I replaced the leather in the cushioned booths that lined both sides of the room.

The deuces and four-tops in the center were spread out spaciously, largely to prevent Gloria Wright, Agnes Sample, Louise Dodge, or Martha Duncan—the new waitress I hired—from bumping into each other or table corners with trays of food and lighting up the dining room with "motherfuckers."

I had entrances and exits put back where you could enter the bar from the parking lot again, or through the door connecting the bar to the dining room.

The old Wurlitzer was rescued from storage and replaced in its familiar corner in the bar. I stocked the jukebox with reminders of what tuneful music was like—for those with no memory of it, which was perhaps two generations.

I loaded it up with Willie and other immortals of country western lyrics and melodies. And I added Frank, Judy, and Satchmo to remind people of what real song-birding was like before it was replaced by howling and screaming.

I brought back the cushioned stools that ran along the bar. Convivial drinkers deserve comfort. The rainbows made drinkers stand or lean.

For reason of nostalgia I had saved Juanita's list of beverages that she kept tacked on a wall in the bar. It reads:

Scotch—Junior, Curtis.

Whiskey—Jack, Crown, Beam.

Vodka—Potato Only.

Juniper Juice—Martini Glass for Sissies.

Beer—Long Bud, Coors Lifeless.

Wine—Red and White.

It went back on a wall, but in a frame this time.

I searched but couldn't find an old Turf King pinball machine like the one we spent too much time gambling on in high school and college.

Naturally I reinstalled the large sign on the tall post on the corner saying you had arrived at: "Herb Macklin's Restaurant & Bar—Chicken Fried Steaks."

I hired back as many of the old staff as cared to return, which was everybody but Mildred Lawson, a waitress. Mildred took a job on a cruise ship that had yet to roll over in a storm.

I moved Bernice Hardy from energetic waitress to manager and cashier. I gave Will Vinson, the chief cook, a super raise and made him our food and beverage manager to go along with his other duties. I didn't forget to boost the pay of Will's kitchen and bar costars, Opal Parker and Sugar Richards.

"This is fine," Sugar said. "*Fine.* Opal, gal, you and me goin' shoppin'."

Nyla Macklin took my money and moved to some bay in Florida to find a new husband, preferably a gentleman who didn't have an oxygen tube in his nose. She said the portable oxygen tank might soon replace the gator as Florida's state bird.

* * * * *

WHEN I was putting the staff together I wondered if I'd made a mistake hiring Bobby Downs as a handyman. He'd begged for the job, saying it was what Herb would have wanted.

I did this knowing that Bobby was familiar to every detective in the city as a "police character." Bobby had been arrested for hot checks, credit card theft, shoplifting, and mugging, but he'd never done time. Crowded court dockets.

I admit Bobby was good at repairing things. Everything from a plumbing problem to an automobile that was sick under the hood. I agreed to let him keep his job as a bagman for Montana Slim. He swore it wouldn't interfere with his duties at the restaurant.

My kindness was repaid two months after Herb's was back in business and doing plenty okay among lovers of good food, good drinks, and intellectual conversation.

The repayment came in the form of a 4 a.m. phone call from Will.

Will said, "Tommy Earl, we been broke into. But it's all right. I done caught the turd-head. He say to call you, not the police."

"Why did he say to call me?"

"Cause you know him. We all do. It's Bobby Downs."

"*Bobby Downs?*"

"Sure enough is," Will said. "I was spendin' the night on my cot. I had work to catch up on. I heard a noise. Bobby broke in from up on the roof."

"Why would he say to call me instead of the cops?"

"He say you'll understand."

"I'll understand why he was trying to *rob* me?"

"That's what he say. I caught him jackin' around in the drawers underneath the register in the dining room. I expect he was lookin' for the cash box. Bobby so dumb he don't know Bernice always take the money home at night so she can make the bank deposit on her way to work in the morning."

I said, "I'll get there quick as I can. Will, remind me to have security cameras installed immediately. Two in the bar, three in the dining room. What's Bobby doing now?"

Will said, "Right now this minute? Right now he tied down in a chair and cryin' like a little kid. That's when he ain't lookin' at the Ruger .38 I got pointed at his dick."

It was no surprise that Will had a license to carry. Everybody in Texas carried a concealed handgun. All you had to do was pass muster with the Texas Department of Public Safety. I'd learned how to use my Glock .19 at a firing range. Olivia was armed. In her job, she was forced to walk through a lot of dark parking lots. She kept a Smith and Wesson .38 in her purse. She was licensed and learned to use it at gun school.

Bobby Downs was a high school dropout, as were Dorito Bracy and Red Fuqua. All three went to Arlington Heights High School, but somehow forgot to graduate. I'd asked Bobby why he and the other two didn't play football for the Yellow Jackets. They looked fit.

"We tried," he said. "But they wanted you to practice every day. That's bullshit, man."

I said, "You could have earned a letter jacket. Something to be proud of."

Bobby said, "Red Fuqua stole one from somebody. It was easier. But he never wore it to school. It could be detrected."

Detrected.

Will said Bobby, Dorito, and Red were the three dumbest white boys he'd ever known.

When I arrived Bobby was in the chair with his head in his hands, struggling not to cry me a river.

I said, "Bobby, you asshole. You want to know the truly sad part? You have no excuse. I don't give a damn if your mama was a drunk and your daddy ran off somewhere when you were a little kid. You were born with the greatest advantage in the world. You were born a citizen of the United States with all the opportunities that come with it."

He said, "Tommy Earl, I'm sorry what I did, but you have to hear the whole story. There's more to it than you think."

"What important detail am I missing? How you broke in from up on the red tile roof?"

"It's not all my fault."

"It's not? Well, let me tell you what is. Five to ten years in the Huntsville state prison. That's all I know."

"Tommy Earl, I needed the cash to keep from getting' kilt."

"What are you talking about?"

He went back to a sob, and said, "I had this bag of money, close to a grand. I was delivering it to a client for Slim. But I made a bad decision. I thought I'd use it to make some coin for myself. I drove to the WinStar casino. It's up there past Gainesville across the Oklahoma border."

"I know where it is."

"I was unlucky, is what happened. I got this urge to go all-in on a full house, and ... "

"Let me guess. Some donkey had four of a kind."

Bobby said, "See, if it wasn't for that, none of the rest would have happened. Slim wouldn't be so hot he'd want to kill me, and I wouldn't have to ask if I can borrow the money from you to pay him back."

"You're asking me for a *loan*?"

"I'm trying to stay alive. Slim ain't known for his kindness and understanding when it comes to money. I've heard about the dude he put in a concrete suit and dumped into Lake Worth."

"That's an old story—and Slim was never arrested."

"They found the body."

"Yeah. Somebody's body."

"Well, hell, Tommy Earl. The body didn't put concrete on itself. You gonna call the cops on me? I'll do anything to make it up to you. Herb would forgive me. I know he would."

I said, "So a loan from me is how you'll handle this with Slim?"

"I got nowhere else to go."

"Jesus," I said to myself.

"I know you don't want to see me get kilt. You can take half my salary every week. I know Herb would do it."

"How much are we talking about?"

"Right at eight hundred and sixty-five dollars."

I glanced at Will. "What do you think?"

Will said, "I'd rather shoot him in the dick."

Bobby yelled, "Come on, Will!"

I let Bobby off and loaned him the money to keep him from possibly coming to bodily harm. I guess you have to say I helped Bobby out because I knew what it was like to make mistakes in my own youth.

10.

THE DETAILS for the reunion began to dominate my thinking after Herb's was restored. I knew it wouldn't be a success unless I made every out-of-towner I wanted to invite sign in blood—or cream gravy—that they would be here.

I started with Billy Clyde Puckett and Barbara Jane Bookman, the restaurant's best-known graduates. They were essential. Through high school and college they did their homework in the bar at Herb's—when they weren't challenging the pinball machine.

It was springtime and our country was sliding deep into the millennium. Big Ed was convinced that this period in our history would be remembered as a time when presumably intelligent parents tolerated the demands of their spoiled, tattooed, body-pierced, chirping-voiced children.

I refer to kids who graduate from college and expect to be offered a starting salary of $200,000 for doing nothing. And when that doesn't happen, they move back home, demand a new car, ten of the latest Playstations, and apply for welfare.

"One of these days," Big Ed said, "there won't be anybody available to sell shirts and ties."

I scheduled the reunion before football season, when Billy Clyde wouldn't be busy sharing his wisdom on TV regarding all things NFL.

Barbara Jane was at the house on Long Island when I reached her on her cell. She said the reunion sounded like fun and I could count on them coming. They hadn't been back for a while. It would be a chance to visit with her folks.

She said, "Daddy's reached ninety, you know?"

I said, "Your mother is lovely and kind as ever. Big Ed is spry and active. He dresses up to come to the office every day. He likes to talk about things."

Barbara Jane said, "I know how Daddy will want to take his leave one day."

"How's that?'

"He'll be sitting a well. The blowout preventer will fail. There'll be an explosion. A big black geyser will shoot into the sky like they did in the old days. He'll raise his arms, holler 'Zip-a-dee-do-dah,' signal a touchdown, do a little dance, and topple over."

I said, "Nothing would please him more."

Barbara Jane and Billy Clyde lived in two homes—the Fifth Avenue apartment in Manhattan and the two-story house in the Hamptons. The Hamptons house was well-appointed and comfortable, but it was nowhere near a part of the area where you found a Windsor Castle lurking behind every row of hedges, trees, or tennis courts.

Olivia and I had visited them twice out there. Barbara Jane made the trip easy. A friend of hers who was well-positioned at a Hollywood studio sent a company Citation X for us. The pilots picked us up at Meacham Field, Fort Worth's first airport, which dated back to 1925. It's where American Airlines was founded. We were dropped off at Islip on Long Island in what seemed like a jiffy.

Those trips reminded me of a Willie Nelson song: "Life Don't Owe Me a Living but a Lear and a Limo Ain't Bad."

Barbara Jane explained that they were spending less time in the city now.

"I used to love Manhattan," she said. "We have great memories from our days of living in the city when Billy Clyde was Red Grange. But it's become filthier and more expensive than ever. Dinner at a popular restaurant that once cost $90 for two now costs $600 for two. How did that happen?

"You have to be nimble today when you stroll out of your apartment. You run the risk of getting pan-handled by an eighth-grade dropout, shot by a gang member, or pissed on by a derelict.

"People still support the theater, God knows why. A hit show on Broadway today is a tenth revival of *Hello, Dolly,* only this time they'll be doing it in Arabic."

As for the Hamptons, I don't know whether Billy Clyde and Barbara Jane live in a forest or a pasture. It was easy for me to confuse the Sagaponacks with the Amagansetts, the Water Mills with the Lily Ponds. It happened that Barbara Jane and Billy Clyde preferred a country lane to a shopping village, a lawn over a swimming pool, and wood-burning fireplaces over a beach.

I've said, "Why don't you guys live in a town like Bridgehampton? It's not a problem to find, and I can pronounce it."

Barbara Jane said, "It would be too easy to track us down."

"Who, me?"

"No, them."

"Who's them?"

"The time bandits," she said.

* * * * *

OVER THE years Barbara Jane had gone from a recognizable fashion model to a movie actress to an independent filmmaker. She'd been told many times in Hollywood that "every movie is a Western." Granted, it was difficult to think of Katharine Hepburn and Spencer Tracy, or Cary Grant and Grace Kelly, as old cowhands, but she made a Western anyway. Wrote it and directed it.

She was in the process of editing *Remember Goliad!* when I called.

"That's the title?" I said.

She said, "Everybody remembers the Alamo—John Wayne was there, right? But nobody remembers Goliad, even though it was half of the battle cry at San Jacinto. . . . 'Remember the Alamo, remember Goliad!'"

"I know *that*," I said. "Goliad was the mission where Col. James Fannin and 350 of his men were massacred by orders of Santa Anna, the president of Mexico and general of the army."

"The massacre is in my movie."

I said, "Our guys were outnumbered when they fought the Mexicans to a standstill in a battle at some creek. But they ran out of food, water, and ammo and surrendered when they were promised they'd be fed and treated honorably as prisoners of war. But instead they were marched to Goliad, lined up, and shot by a firing squad. Those who survived the rifle fire were stabbed to death. Santa Anna was a fun guy."

Barbara Jane said, "I'm making a feature, not a documentary. The fictitious hero I've created is a young man from Georgia who moves to Texas to be a rancher, a landowner, and he volunteers to fight for Texas independence in General Sam Houston's army."

"He becomes a hero, I'll wager."

She said, "He's a fighting devil at the Siege of San Antonio . . . with General Stephen F. Austin, James Fannin, Ben Milam, and 'Deaf' Smith, who was Sam Houston's most reliable scout."

"San Antonio was our first big win," I said.

She said, "My guy is with Fannin and the others when they surrender at the Battle of Coleto Creek. It's a fact that thirty-four of Fannin's men escaped from the Goliad massacre. My hero is one of them. He slogs his way across the prairie and joins up with General Houston's army."

"He'd better, or the movie's over."

"Want to hear the rest, wise guy?"

"I know what happens. He marries the Rose of San Antone or the Yellow Rose of Texas. There are choices in life."

"Not yet," Barbara Jane said. "He joins Colonel Mirabeau Lamar's cavalry and kills his share of the enemy at the Battle of San Jacinto. Sam Houston's army wipes out close to 1,300 soldiers in the Mexican army. The next day my guy's with two other soldiers when they capture Santa Anna. He was trying to escape. They find him hiding in a ditch."

"In real life our guys should have carved him up with his own sword."

"My guy is too noble, like the ones in real life. He stops the others from carving up the general with his own sword, as you put it. He convinces them that Santa Anna ought to be sent back to Mexico to live the rest of his days in disgrace. His people can watch the bastard wind up among history's great failures. They don't say 'loser.' Nobody said 'loser' then."

I asked, "What's the actor's name who plays your hero?"

She said, "I yanked him out of a TV series. You wouldn't know the name if I told you. This is the millennium, and you're not fourteen years old."

11.

BILLY CLYDE was too busy to talk on the phone. He was outdoors playing with their newly acquired doggies. A female Welsh Corgi and a King Charles Spaniel. The doggies were apparently bearing up well under the names Barbara Jane gave them.

Gisele and Tom.

I understood why Billy Clyde didn't want to talk. Talking was his profession now. Talking on TV became his job after his football career was over. Except, of course, for the season he spent as general manager of the Tornadoes.

It was no mystery why TV wanted Billy Clyde. He was among the most decorated football players in history. He was "the Paydirt Panther" as an All-State running back at Paschal. He was "the Horned Frog Hurricane" as a two-time All-America running back at TCU. And he became the "Galloping Giant," a seven-time All-Pro when he delivered the pigskin for the New York Giants.

Like hundreds of others, I was outraged when he was gypped out of the Heisman in college. Careless voters went for a Notre

Dame halfback on a team that played a weaker schedule than Franklin & Marshall.

Twelve years of taking licks in the pros was an amazing achievement for Billy Clyde if you consider that the average life of an NFL running back is four seasons. Yet he lasted eight years longer, and soon after retirement he was inducted into the College Football Hall of Fame and the NFL Hall of Fame.

He somehow found time to cowrite a book while he was helping the Giants win that Super Bowl. He collaborated on it with Jim Tom Pinch, another local regular, who had been hired by the *Sports Magazine* in New York City.

Every athlete who writes a book needs a mechanic. I reveal this in case you think every famous athlete knows how to type.

They both still complain about the title. The genius publisher insisted on what he called the "marketable title" of *Billy Clyde Puckett Talks Football.*

Billy Clyde had argued strongly for his title: *Have You Pissed in a Bottle for the Trainer Today?*

He estimates the publisher's title cost him a million in sales.

* * * * *

BILLY CLYDE'S first job in TV was the color commentator on an NFL game every Sunday. He worked with Roundy McGill, a well-known play-by-play broadcaster who did other sports in other seasons. Roundy was held in high regard by sponsors for never saying a critical word on the air about an athlete, coach, manager, owner, city, fan, seat-cushion, or bag of popcorn.

Billy Clyde's role was to make informative comments, to which Roundy McGill would say, "Right you are, Puckett Man."

Billy Clyde no longer does games. He grew tired of the travel. Weary of trying to find something complimentary to say about the sorry NFL teams with stingy owners. He had enough stroke to name his job. That's how he became a studio panelist in New York working with three other retired immortals on pre-game, halftime, and post-game telecasts.

The other panelists were W. H. "Waffle House" Hunter, who had set passing records for the Broncos, Bengals, and Chiefs, and two former NFL coaches who had won Super Bowls: Frank "Foggy" McCorkle and Dudley "Dough-Pop" Dillard.

Billy Clyde assured me that his TV job wasn't coal-mining, but he couldn't say things like all the assistant coaches are too fat.

"Ask me a question," he said. "I'll show you how easy it is."

I thought about it, and said, "Do you agree that the Seattle Seahawks aren't what they used to be?"

"They definitely settled for too many field goals last season. They can use a coordinator who is better acquainted with the Red Zone."

I grinned.

"Ask me something else."

I came up with, "Do you think the Dallas Cowboys will ever be what the Cowboys once were?"

"The Cowboys know what the Cowboys are all about. You'll never see the Cowboys headed in the wrong direction."

I grinned again.

"Fire another one at me."

"Coaches seem to be shifting from a drop-back passer to a duel-threat guy. What's your take on that?"

"A coach sometimes has to stick his toe in the water and let it tell him what a quick fix can do for him. Gimme one more."

I went with, "Do you think the Detroit Lions will ever grow tired of being called 'the Same Old Lions?' They haven't had a great team since Bobby Layne."

"Things are changing with that franchise. They're sending a signal to the division. I like it that they expect the wide receiver they drafted to earn his starter-money."

"Starter-money?" I laughed. "You're killing me."

Billy Clyde said, "It doesn't matter what I say on the air. No player or coach knows more about the game than the devoted fan."

"Like the Draft-niks?"

Billy Clyde said, "Worse. The tweets I get are something else. One guy hopes the coach of the Cowboys will die in his sleep. Another guy prays the Miami quarterback will get kidnapped and disappear in Cuba. A woman in DC says she'll pay $1,000 to pour acid down the throat of the Redskins owner. The best one is the guy in San Francisco who said he'd become a suicide bomber if he thought he could get near enough to the 49ers team plane."

"Love a sports fan," I said.

Billy Clyde said, "They keep me entertained."

12.

SHAKE TILLER, it seemed to me, worked at being a puzzle to the rest of Western Civilization. I'd swear he took pride in it. He was a hellacious football player, the best pass receiver I've ever seen—speed, hands, moves, the complete package—but he didn't like football.

I should say that differently. Shake loved the competition, the game days, but he didn't like authority figures. Coaches, for instance.

Actually Shake didn't like any authority figure. He swore that every lecture he heard from a teacher or a university professor was so boring it would put a trapeze artist to sleep in mid-flight of a triple without a net.

When Shake and Billy Clyde were teammates in high school, college, and the pros, Shake thought every coach was a blight on the sport. In order of appearance, they would be "Bucko" Thomas at Paschal, "Chew" Mosley at TCU, and Shoat Cooper with the Giants.

Billy Clyde remembers hearing Shake say to the coach of the Giants at practice, "Your name fits you perfect, Shoat. But

I can't decide whether it's because you look like a pig or you think like a pig."

That might be the kindest thing Shake ever said to an authority figure. He hated the babble that accompanied workout drills, film study, team meetings, chalkboard sessions, pre-game pep talks, halftime talks, and post-game talks.

Shake insisted the game wasn't complicated. It was blocking and tackling, throwing and catching, running and not getting caught.

When we were hanging out at Herb's I've never forgotten what I learned from him about football in one remark. He said:

"Any athlete who has to be *motivated* to give his best on the football field should switch to dominoes—he can sit down the whole game."

*****

THE FRIENDSHIP involving Billy Clyde, Barbara Jane, and Shake dated back to grade school. They were closer than paint on a wall. A major requirement was a sense of humor. They had other friends, but I was the only one to crash their inner circle. It was like winning a three-team parlay without the help of Alabama and Ohio State.

The long period when Shake and Barbara Jane were an item—from the fifth grade through college and the pros—Billy Clyde played best friend.

In later years he confessed to me that he had secretly been in love with Barbara Jane his whole life but kept it to himself. It might have damaged the friendship of the three, and he treasured that more.

But Billy Clyde knew Shake never loved Barbara Jane as much as she thought he did. There were hints of it when Shake became fascinated with such questions as *Can Relevance Be*

Meaningful, Does Matter Care if the Mind Sits on It, and *Why Are Recreational Drugs Illegal?* Shake could find a burning issue on any city block.

Billy Clyde in the meantime would hook up with a fun-loving lady to "take the pressure off." He never stooped to a Dirty Leg, but he would take out the babes who dressed "too-tight-and-too-cheap," as Barbara Jane categorized them.

Shake played three more seasons after the Super Bowl triumph, but that Giants team never won anything other than a division title. T. J. Lambert retired to coach, and there went the defensive unit. Shoat Cooper retired to his Arkansas farm. A series of young head coaches came and went. Some smart, most dumb, all of them arrogant.

Then came the day in the early nineties when Shake summoned Billy Clyde and Barbara Jane to what he said would be "an important meeting."

They gathered at Hemlock's, a dreary bar in the Village near Shake's apartment where no one would know them—or care to know them.

It was the day Shake broke the news that he was retiring from football immediately. He intended to travel the world and give considerable thought to what he was going to do with the rest of his life.

Billy Clyde shared highlights of the meeting with me.

Barbara Jane's predictable reaction to Shake's announcement was to dismiss it as a joke.

She said to Shake, "Does this mean our wedding in Nantucket is off? I'll have to inform my bridesmaids at Wellesley."

"I'm serious," Shake said.

"Since when?" Billy Clyde said.

"Good question," Barbara Jane, glancing at Billy Clyde.

Shake said, "I've never been out of the country. I've seen nothing but locker rooms and hotels in my life. I want to visit foreign countries. See what's there, up close and personal."

Barbara Jane said, "Great, when do we start?"

"There's no 'we' in this deal."

"Are you saying I'm not invited?"

"I have to do this on my own, babe."

"You have to do this on *your own?*"

"It's time to make a decision about the rest of my life."

"Say something, Billy Clyde!"

Billy Clyde looked away.

"I'm not joking, Barb," said Shake.

"Why alone, Shake, if it's not impolite of me to ask?"

"Do I detect a pissed-offness in your tone?"

"I'm *hurt*, damn it."

"I don't want to hurt you. I want you to understand."

Barbara Jane said, "I'll try. After you explain what I'm supposed to do while you're gone, other than sit home and crochet a quilt?"

Shake said, "You have a career, B. J. You're a famous model. Hollywood wants to make you an actress. No telling where things will lead. Football is out of my future. I am not going to wind up a coach or assistant coach in some rural part of America where everybody gathers at Arby's. I know there's a better future for me, but I've got to make it happen. I think I may try to write."

Billy Clyde spoke up. "Foreign countries, huh? I'll tell you what you'll find in foreign counties."

"What?"

"A bunch of ruins."

"How would you know? You've never been anywhere either."

"I thumbed through a copy of *National Geographic* one day when I was in the dentist's office."

"Did you see any ruins?"

"One in the Congo. It had a yellow arch on top."

Barbara Jane sighed heavily.

Then she said, "Shake Tiller, do you know what you've become? A goddamn dope-head. I've tried to think it was one of your phases—like trying to learn how to play chess with those geezers in Washington Square. You're on the weed or sniffing powder every day. Your mind is the most valuable thing you have. Why do you want to jack around with it?"

"Weed is a form of enhancement. Coke is just speed."

"Jesus, you're smarter than that. Can you give me an answer that doesn't bubble over with stupidity?"

Shake said, "Hey, I didn't ask you guys here to have an argument. We're talking about my life. You guys have choices. But you want to act like I'm a criminal because I like to experiment with something I can grow in my own yard."

"You don't *have* a yard! You live in a New York apartment. And how do you excuse the cocaine?"

"Maybe I want to see what made everybody so witty in the thirties."

Barbara Jane said, "Billy Clyde, help me out here."

Billy Clyde said, "A man's got to do what a man's got to do."

Barbara Jane stood up. "This is bullshit. I'm outta here."

Shake hopped up. "Hold on a minute."

Barbara Jane jerked away. "I'm the best lady you'll ever know and you don't even realize it. Send me a postcard, Shake. You have my address—unless you've smoked it!"

And she was gone.

13.

SHAKE SPENT close to two years in Europe, which can seem like an eternity at a certain stage of your life. However, it was enough time for Barbara Jane and Billy Clyde to realize they had fancied each other all along but had carefully avoided the issue.

When Shake left on his journey in search of truth, beauty, and typing paper, Barbara Jane went through stages—anger, confusion, sadness. Eventually the friendship with Billy Clyde nosedived into passion. When that occurs, life dictates that you can call in an air strike, but nothing will stop you from humming a favorite tune as you stroll down the avenue.

They had begun to have dinner four or five nights a week. It was like they didn't know anyone else, except they didn't care to. It was during one of those evenings when Billy Clyde said, "I've been holding this in for too many years—I just have to throw it out there, no matter what happens. I've been hopelessly in love with you forever, Barb."

Barbara Jane said, "You have no idea how long I've wanted to hear you say that to me."

"Dare we make it official?"

"I happen to have it at the top of my wish list."

Billy Clyde and Barbara Jane were married at poolside of Big Ed's home in Westover Hills, if you want to call something a home that has a moat, a tennis court, a bent grass putting green, a guest cottage, and an Olympic-size swimming pool shaped like a Horned Frog. I'm not lying to anybody.

An intimate group of Bookman friends were invited to the wedding. Olivia and I were among them. The high-water mark of the ceremony was when Rev. O. D. ("Dog") Dawkins, a preacher and Big Ed's friend, asked who gives this woman? The booming voice of Big Ed said:

"Her mother, her father, and the Fightin' Horned Frogs of Texas Christian University!"

* * * * *

BILLY CLYDE and Barbara Jane kept up with Shake through his postcards, which were not what you would classify as regular. Two or three months would pass.

They did hear from him after they married. Shake read a story about it in the *International Herald Tribune*, and he wrote to them, "I'm glad you guys saw the light. I know you won't mess it up."

That postcard came from Athens with a picture of a ruin on it. Another card came from Rome with a picture of a different ruin on it. He'd read in the *Herald Trib* about Billy Clyde gaining 203 yards from scrimmage while weaving his way to four touchdowns against the Eagles.

That postcard said, "Old 23, we'll never forget him."

Shake Tiller humor. Billy Clyde always wore No. 22.

Shake lived for a while in Rome and Paris—long enough to examine most of the ruins—then longer in London. The London stop was where he devoted three months to an affair with an attractive divorcee, Alexis Wells, who'd been left well-fixed financially with a townhouse on the Thames.

They'd met at Fortnum & Mason in a food aisle. Things went smoothly until the night at home when Alexis drank too much red and cursed him bitterly for not liking a sporting event she made him attend.

It was the annual "boat race." The deadly battle of eights in the Oxford and Cambridge crew race of four miles on the Thames. Maybe things would have gone better if Shake hadn't said the race looked more to him like a day in the park.

On another evening Alexis, loaded again on the red, cursed him for not liking the Shakespeare comedy she'd dragged him to see in a theater that was about to crumble from age. Shake said he liked Shakespeare plays when the actors had sword fights. That only drove her into another rage.

Which led to the moment when Shake said, "Forsooth," moved out, and scratched one English divorcee. It would be easier to understand cricket.

A journalist Shake met in The Punch Tavern, a Fleet Street pub that was almost as old as the theater, suggested he try the Cotswolds, if he could afford it, and wanted to go somewhere to write.

Shake not only visited the Cotswolds, he settled there. He bought a car in London and toured all seven counties and observed so many picturesque villages he had trouble deciding where to hole up with his portable typewriter.

He chose Bourton-on-the-Water. It had slightly more charm than other villages he'd seen. Stone cottages, thatched roofs, rock walls, a knoll, a market. All that.

The body of water was the Windrush River, but in his cards and letters Shake referred to the town as "Mutton-on-Avon."

Shake talked the manager of a little hotel into renting him a two-room suite with a private bath and a view of a cobblestone street. He could stay as long as he wished. That's how the Old Bridge Inn became his home.

Such news required a letter from him. He confessed to Barbara Jane and Billy Clyde that he'd found the perfect place to write. Dozens of pubs were available for food and beverages. There were other villages within hiking distance. Other rivers and streams available if a man wanted to plop down, stare at them, and think. The hills were alive with synonyms and metaphors.

Months later they received the letter informing them that he was off drugs completely. Was this a joke?

No, thank goodness.

Shake became convinced that a recreational drug was a danger. Its merry path took you from smoke to sniff to needle to death. He decided to live longer. Weed had become too powerful anyhow. A man could mummify himself. That was never what he intended. He had only liked to burn one now and then, giggle at something on the TV, and hope there were some Mallomars left in the cabinet.

All on his own, he became convinced that drugs were part of a plot by commies inside and outside our own government to weaken, deaden, and do away with the America we were raised to love and respect. He was certain of this.

"Call me a patriot," he wrote to Billy Clyde and Barbara Jane.

It was while he was cooped up in England that Shake wrote his first book, *The Average Man's History of the World*. He found the name of a literary agent—Shep Burns—in a magazine, and sent it off. The book not only attracted an American publisher, it became a surprising best-seller.

That achievement was in spite of a barrage of savage reviews by critics who, according to Shake, never liked a book unless it was written by a limping Russian dwarf recalling his years in the gulag.

In his book Shake passes judgement on events and characters that have been twisted from culture to culture, as in "our culture is superior to your culture."

A few examples:

The Napoleonic Wars in truth were fought to determine whether the Brits or the French wore the funniest hats.

Our Civil War wasn't about slavery. It was a land-grab. The savvy old North peered into the future and saw that America was going to need golf resorts in warm-weather climates.

People of the Great Depression introduced rags for clothing, never guessing that rock musicians and teenage girls would revive the look thirty years later.

Hitler was a bad guy, no argument there. But if he were here to defend himself he'd argue that he possessed many fine traits. He loved dogs. He loved art. He loved classical music. He loved women. And he was actually pro life—at least for the people who were born naturally blond.

Football? A business venture that followed cattle drives.

Best Drink of all-time: the root beer float.

Cutting horses: Where rich people go to play cowboy.

Is it Hungro-Austria or Austro-Hungary?

Why does Java keep all the best typhoons for itself?

Two things are guaranteed to make a Russian laugh: One, give him a pair of American jeans, or two, let him shoot a German.

Stop complaining about taxes, unless you don't want us to have an Army and Navy.

Vietnam? The most fun any door-gunner could have.

The over-romanticized sixties? Even ugly people could get laid.

Shake had written most of the book on his portable typewriter, but he finished it on a laptop computer, which he said was God's gift to writers.

The best thing Shake's book did was bring him home. The home he selected was a rental cottage in Hollywood. His book's success had led to an advance on a novel that came with a movie tie-in. He had been grinding on the novel for months. Not surprisingly, it was about a football player. So far, he was struggling with it. He was only satisfied with the title: *Stud Lovable*.

While Shake was overseas, I watched Barbara Jane become a movie actor who hated it—she was only good playing herself. And I watched Billy Clyde retire as a gridiron hero and become an NFL analyst on TV.

Shake arrived in the States as Barbara Jane was finishing up her last scene in her last movie, *Melancholy Baby*.

It almost didn't get finished. She kept refusing to say lines in the script written by "a bearded elf."

Billy Clyde was on the set the day Barbara Jane said to the writer, "I will not say, 'Love is like a work of art—it takes an artist to do it right.' I feel like I've heard that somewhere, or read it somewhere. And allow me to be clear one more time. I would never say that if I fucking *believed* it."

14.

SHAKE'S RETURN coincided with the miracle of the West Texas Tornadoes.

Barbara Jane and Billy Clyde were happy to have him back—and clean. They made him a partner in Barbara Jane's film company, End Zone Productions. I was exceedingly pleased when he arrived at Gully Creek in time for the playoffs and the Super Bowl.

At a Tornadoes practice, Shake said, "They look awfully slow, Tommy Earl. Kind of small, too. How'd they beat anybody?"

I said, "The same way you guys did. Character and conditioning."

When he discovered that Gully Creek was near the Brazos River, he planned to find a way to work the Brazos into *Stud Lovable*. I asked him why? Did the Brazos play a part in the story?

He said, "I like the word. There are words readers like to say out loud to themselves. Brazos is that kind of word. *Brazos.*"

I could only offer his remark a nod.

As delighted as I was to see Shake back home, I couldn't have been more delighted than Shake when he met Kelly Sue Woodley, the babe Billy Clyde brought on board as his assistant general manager of the Tornadoes.

Billy Clyde discovered Kelly Sue on a trip to Fort Worth to recruit T. J. Lambert for head coach of the Tornadoes. T. J. was all done lifting TCU out of waste management and into gridiron glory.

T. J. demanded that Billy Clyde meet him to discuss the job in a hideout saloon largely known to west-side gentlemen who didn't care to be seen daytime drunk at the country clubs.

Kelly Sue owned and bartended the establishment her parents left her. The original name of the bar was the Sunset Tavern, but she changed it to He's Not Here. She preferred something funny. The only food she offered was from the pot of butter beans she made every day with cornbread sticks. When that was gone, there were salted peanuts.

It had taken Billy Clyde two long afternoons in He's Not Here to persuade T. J. to take the coaching job. And it was in those visits that he became impressed with Kelly Sue. Her smarts, energy, humor, and looks. The result was that he talked her into finding a trustworthy fellow to manage the joint for her.

Billy Clyde didn't have to worry about Barb being jealous of Kelly Sue's looks. Barbara Jane was secure in her own falling-down beauty. The ladies met when Barbara Jane dropped in on Gully Creek for a surprise visit.

Kelly Sue said, "It's all over town that you and Shake Tiller at one time were tangled up in a love knot."

"I was for years," Barbara Jane replied. "Until I discovered he was more in love with himself."

Kelly Sue said, "That is so inconvenient, don't you think?"

Shake was introduced to Kelly Sue when she walked into the GM's office while Billy Clyde and Shake were having a beer and talking about old times.

Kelly Sue said, "My God, it's Shake Tiller! I've been in love with the guy on that book jacket since the first time I saw it."

Shake said, "Did you bother to read the book?"

"Every word. I was thrilled when Scarlett and Rhett patched things up."

Shake stood up to meet her properly. He was six foot three. She was five foot six.

Shake took her hand as he said, "Want to form the perfect race?"

Kelly Sue howled with laughter.

They've been together ever since.

* * * * *

WHEN I reached Shake on his smartphone to alert him about the reunion, and how it wouldn't be the same without his esteemed presence, he said, "Will I know anybody there besides you?"

I said, "Billy Clyde and Barbara Jane are signed up. I don't know how many regulars you'll remember. I'm still working on the invitation list."

"Is your chicken fried steak as good as Herb's was?"

I said, "You're asking me if our chicken fried steak is *good*? Hey, buddy. Go in the front and have it for dinner, go out the back and eat the garbage."

"That's a hell of a selling point," Shake said. "I'll be there anyhow."

15.

IT WAS in that awkward period before I took rich that I watched Juanita Hutchins climb in her Chevy pickup, wave goodbye to Herb's bar after fifteen years, and head for Nashville and her new life as a country music songwriter. Slick Henderson didn't ride shotgun. He followed her in his '79 mint-condition Pontiac Firebird Trans Am. Juanita never looked back, and she's never gone pop.

Juanita and Slick were in love by then. They were married quietly before they left town. Slick handed over the management and part ownership of his Exxon station to a trustworthy friend, Snap Rogers, a home-grown second baseman who'd done a stint in the show with the Yankees. Slick appointed himself Juanita's agent and business manager.

Juanita had said, "Is that wise, Slick? You and me don't know anything about the dealings of show-biz."

Slick said, "I know the two biggest things. I know how to say no until the price is right . . . and I know that nobody ever wants anything until somebody else also wants it."

She said, "I'm taking in Old Jeemy as a minor partner. He'll be helpful on the air. He has lots of friends in country music, and they're known to scratch one another's back."

"That'll give me something else to do," said Slick. "Keep a sharp eye on Old Jeemy Williams."

Since Juanita was a young girl she'd written country songs for fun. She played the self-taught guitar well enough to get by, and once in a while she'd try out one of her songs on a customer in the bar, hoping her lyrics might hit a nerve.

Old Jeemy, the most popular country DJ in Fort Worth and surrounding territories, listened to a couple of numbers one afternoon while he lapped up a chicken fried steak sitting at the bar. He thought her songs were promising, and he would try to talk his good friend Willie Nelson into recording them.

Big names like Willie normally only record their own songs, but they'll do another writer's effort if it appeals to them. In the past Willie had recorded work written by Shel Silverstein, Bob Wills, Waylon Jennings, Kris Kristofferson, and the team of Ed and Patsy Bruce, to name a few of the successful.

Willie told Juanita he would always be grateful to Patsy Cline for kick-starting his career when she recorded "Crazy." The music world lost as great a singing voice as it would ever hear when Patsy Cline was killed at the age of thirty in the crash of a private plane.

Juanita said, "Well, Jeemy, if you can make the Willie thing happen, it will certify you as a truly great American and wonderful human being."

Old Jeemy got it done. Willie first recorded Juanita's "Midnight Songs."

Too many nights turn into dawns,
Too many rights turn into wrongs,
There were too many midnight songs.

When that became a hit, Willie did Juanita's "Baja Oklahoma."

It's a roundup stirring memories of the rough-and-tumble days,
It's a detour off the freeway to see where you were raised.

That one didn't do as well, but by then Juanita and Slick were hauling ass to Tennessee.

Old Jeemy laid out a plan for them in Nashville. It wasn't complicated. Go to "headquarters," as he referred to Tootsie's Orchid Lounge. "Don't waste your time in another honky tonk."

He explained that Jimmy Rodgers, "the Father of Country Music," and Bob Wills, "the King of Western Swing," were the only two giants of country music that weren't discovered in Nashville. Tootsie's, he related, is conveniently located across the alley from a treasured hunk of real estate, the Ryman Auditorium, original home of the Grand Ole Opry.

"I love Jimmy Rodgers," Juanita has said. "I can't count the times I've felt like I was 'a thousand miles away from home, waitin' on a train.'"

Old Jeemy said, "Tootsie's is where you find the top producers, arrangers, singers, musicians, and songwriters. The artists start singin' and pickin' at ten in the morning when the joint opens, and they don't stop until closing time, which is 3 a.m. If anybody with an inch of talent is not on one of the three stages at Tootsie's, it's because they ain't learned to crawl yet."

Juanita asked, "How do I get on a stage at Tootsie's so Patsy Cline can come back to life and discover my genius?"

Old Jeemy said, "Slick will figure it out. It's a simple matter of economics."

Those of us who follow Juanita's career know that it didn't take long for her to become a success. Waddy Hills and other established entertainers recorded Juanita's songs. That list included Ray Roy Horn, Vally Lynn Burk, Keith Gerth, Joe Dean Hicks, and Betty Kay Ponder.

After six years of succeeding as a songwriter, Juanita gave in to the urging of Old Jeemy and Slick and became a performer.

But not the kind you'd find on the stage at a country or pop concert nowadays.

When I mentioned that Juanita never went pop, I meant she never put on a cowboy hat, appeared in a rhinestone dress, or wore a Goddess of the Jungle costume. And she would never do a song today that passes for popular. By that I mean a song with no melody and lyrics to entertain the brain-damaged.

Like me, lick me, blow me.

As Juanita would say, "*It ain't Singin' in the Rain.*"

But of course a number like that would be tastefully presented with fireworks, thunder storms, cannon fire, fog-machines, a big band, a small band, twenty dancers wriggling around in catsuits.

All of which is what the entertainment industry believes it has to do these days to remain relevant.

In opposition, Juanita became a no-frills entertainer.

It's just her at the mic in a pair of boots, designer jeans, blouse or shirt, with the Martin guitar draped around her neck.

She assembled a group of accomplished musicians to work with her—a rhythm guitar, a bass guitar, a piano man, a drummer, and another rhythm guy who can also handle the Dobro and an acoustic guitar, although not as skillfully as Fort Worth's own T Bone Burnett.

She named the group "Red-Eye Gravy."

Juanita is fortunate to have a unique singing voice. Sort of like you recognize Loretta Lynn when you hear her, but in no way would Juanita compare herself to "the First Lady of Country Music."

Juanita doesn't do many concerts, and picks her spots. Atlanta, Birmingham, Charlotte, Memphis. Mostly cities she can reach in the comfort of her luxury bus.

On stage she spaces out her own songs with those of others that she considers "anthems." Her anthem list includes Cindy Walker's "Goin' Away Party," Emmylou Harris's "I'll Be Your

San Antonio Rose," Loretta's "You Ain't Woman Enough to Take My Man," Elvis on "Are You Lonesome Tonight," Mickey Gilley doing "Someday," Merle Haggard's "Fightin' Side of Me," George Strait's "Right or Wrong," and "Mamas, Don't Let Your Babies Grow Up to be Cowboys," which was immortalized by Willie and Waylon.

* * * * *

WHEN I reached Juanita she was home in the mansion she and Slick were proud of—and why not? It was in Nashville's Belle Meade section. Old South. Elegance. Manicured lawns. Stately trees. Gardens bursting in colors. They had been approved to join Belle Meade Country Club, which they promptly did.

I had interrupted Juanita from working on a song. Which is what she does when she's not cooking a country ham with red-eye gravy and homemade biscuits.

She said, "We got your email about the reunion. We'll be there. We wouldn't miss it."

"Great," I said. "Now if I can dig up Tammye Wynette and George Jones."

"Smart ass," she said. "Do you know Slick plays golf now?"

"Does he play in his grease repellent shirt with the Exxon logo on it?"

"He has a closet stuffed with golf togs. He's not good enough at it to gamble for big money. He tells me he shoots in the low to middle eighties."

"Tell him not to get any better at it. Could be costly."

"He plays with a bunch of old white-haired socialites who don't like to lose more than five dollars."

"I hope Slick doesn't come home and take you through his round."

"He wouldn't bother. I don't know fudge about golf. Only that it takes all day to play it."

"That's why I've never taken it up. Glaciers are faster."

Juanita said, "About the reunion, you know I sneak back to Fort Worth twice a year to visit Grace. She's now in the Nonprofit Clear Fork Assisted Living Facility. I do wonder why they call it 'nonprofit' since they charge me eight thousand dollars a month to keep her there."

Juanita calls Grace the "Mama of Sickness." Grace has invented more diseases than a team of Swedish scientists with microscopes and test tubes. It was her specialty. Grace's friends at the facility are narrowed down to those who discuss and compare diseases with her.

The last time Juanita visited Grace she learned that her mother had decided she didn't want to be cremated. She preferred a burial.

Grace said it will be easier for God to lift her up and take her upstairs when the time comes, although God might risk contamination from one of her diseases. But it would save Juanita the trouble of finding a pot plant for her ashes.

Juanita's song in progress was called "Foolin' Around."

She let me hear a bit of it.

"Foolin' around ain't easy,
It takes more than time.
Got to know who needs pleasin',
Who tells the truth and who's lyin."

* * * * *

JUANITA BROUGHT me up to date on her daughter, Candy. The beautiful daughter was rid of her dope-peddling boyfriend,

Dove Christian. He had done two stretches in Seagoville, a soft-core institution for young men, but now he's doing hard time for murder in the federal penitentiary in Beaumont, Texas, which I hear is the last place you'd compare to a Ritz Carlton.

Dove was handsome, likable, fun for the whole family, but otherwise full of shit. You could add stupid to it. Twice he managed to be caught selling heroin to undercover narcs. One was dressed like a cowhand fresh off a ranch and the other one like a priest. But to reach the Big Indoors he required the use of a claw-head hammer to kill a fellow dealer for stealing money from him.

"You can't let that slide," he said to Candy when she visited him.

Candy was living in Dallas and holding down the best bartender job in the city. It was the bar in the grill room of a new modern hotel in Highland Park on the near-north side. The name of the hotel is The Spot. The grill room had become so chic and popular, the management changed the original name from Scotties to Chic & Pop.

Chic & Pop at The Spot.

Candy let her mother in on the secret that on certain nights, she could pocket over eight hundred dollars in tips.

Juanita said, "I asked her to join us at the reunion but she says she would miss out on too much coin. It's good to see her raking in the loot, but I've got tell you, Tommy Earl. I don't see how any woman can afford enough makeup to live in Dallas."

16.

LIKE ANY successful football coach, T. J. Lambert would be quick to tell you that the trouble with winning is you have to keep doing it or your ass will get fired. It's why T. J. retired a winner. All freckle-faced, fair-skinned, red-headed, six-foot-five, 265 pounds of him. His life today consists of eating, sleeping, riding his bike, and bitching about everything on TV except Fox News.

T. J.'s politics are in line with most football coaches, but he wasn't the greatest quote machine the press had dealt with. Most of his statements were impossible to twist into print. He'd say of an upcoming opponent, "We're gonna hit 'em so hard in their pouches they won't know which bathroom to use."

Two of his statements continue to circulate through computer world.

One. How to survive as a coach in the pros: "Get your team to the playoffs every season, but never win the Super Bowl. Keep your fans hungry."

Two. How to survive as a bigtime college coach: "Go 8-4 every season but win the Toilet Bowl."

T. J. did better than all that. In his first head coaching job he took Southern Miss to a bowl game, which was impossible, and in his farewell coaching job he won the Super Bowl with the Tornadoes.

In between, he guided the Horned Frogs to a piece of the national championship in one poll. But he quoted the words of Bear Bryant: "You only need to win one, then your people can play-like they won 'em all."

This was before the Bowl Championship Series got itself invented to the delight of the five major conferences. Now a school can lose all twelve games in the regular season, year after year, but still rake in millions from TV. Is that sweet enough to make a chancellor dress like a Sinclair dinosaur and dance in the street?

I expected everybody to appreciate T. J.'s thoughts on the world in general, which is why I called him at his retirement home in Horseshoe Bay to remind him about the reunion. He hadn't answered my emails. Probably busy rooting for busted kneecaps on every hate-America buffoon in the country.

Horseshoe Bay is fifty-some miles north of Austin. A spread-out area of mansions worth millions that face a body of water combining Lake Lyndon B. Johnson with a branch of the Colorado River. T. J. and Donna Lou live in one of the two-story houses with the lake for a front yard. Five golf courses are available, but T. J. only rides his bike around them and through them.

* * * * *

T. J. WAS a ferocious competitor as a player. A two-time All-America defensive end at the University of Tennessee. Five years All-Pro with the Giants. A savage hitter. Billy Clyde described him as "the kind of defensive player who had no patience for back-talk."

Tales of T. J.'s lack of patience are preserved in the memories of his teammates, and friends like me.

In the seasons he was with the Giants, he became bothered that he hadn't received a raise in two seasons. He marched into Coach Shoat Cooper's office to discuss it. Everyone on the squad and coaching staff knew that Shoat drank four Dr. Peppers a day and each bottle was laced with a jigger of Jack Daniels.

When Shoat told T. J. he didn't have a raise in the budget at the present time, T. J. picked up the Dr. Pepper off Shoat's desk and chug-a-lugged it down.

As Shoat stared at him speechless, T. J. said, "Sorry about that, Coach, but being underpaid makes me thirsty."

There was the time the Giants were in Chicago for the opening game of the season with the Bears. T. J. and Billy Clyde and two other teammates were downtown the night before the game savoring the delights of Rush, Clark, and State streets.

They were milling around on the sidewalk outside a tavern when Wiley "Wolf Hound" Dusek showed up. Wolf Hound was a rookie linebacker out of Duke. The Bears had chosen him No. 1 in the NFL draft.

Wolf Hound had already made his load that night, which caused him to say to T. J., "You're the badass T. J. Lambert, right? Why don't you and me get it on right now, right here, stink on stink?"

T. J. grinned at him, and said, "Wolfie Boy, you know what?"

Wolf Hound said, "What?"

T. J. said, "I don't have time for your cheap shit."

With that, he quickly grabbed Wolf Hound by his neck and his crotch, lifted him up over his head, and threw him away.

Yeah. Sailed him up in the air six or seven yards down the street.

Wolf Hound Dusek landed on the concrete curb and suffered a torn ACL, a fractured elbow, a broken jaw, and a chronic neck injury. He never played a down of pro ball.

And there was the time the Giants were in Dallas the night before a game with the Cowboys. I met Billy Clyde, Shake, and T. J. in a bar that a player with the Cowboys recommended. It was north of downtown, surrounded by apartments for singles. Supposedly it was a get-lucky joint, as one might have guessed from the name: Exes and Ohs.

I was having a cocktail at the bar with Billy Clyde and Shake when I saw T. J. on the dance floor in a dispute with three muscled-up, mean-looking buzz-cuts covered in tattoos. The argument appeared to be over who was going to dance with a young lady. Suddenly they decided to take the discussion outdoors.

I nudged Billy Clyde and Shake, who had their backs to the dance floor, and said, "T. J. just went outside with three bad-looking dudes. They were having a disagreement over a lady."

Billy Clyde said, "Jesus, T. J. will kill 'em!"

He and Shake spun off their barstools and plowed their way through the crowd to go outside and prevent the mayhem. I followed them.

We arrived before any fists were flying.

"You guys don't know who you're dealing with," Billy Clyde said. "This gentleman right here is Mr. T. J. Lambert of the New York City Football Giants."

"They know that *now*," T. J. said. "They want my autograph. Anybody got a damn pen?"

* * * * *

"**WHAT'S** up, asshole?"

That's how T. J. answers the phone if it's not the governor of Texas or his wife Donna Lou.

"Just checking in," I said. "Making sure you're set for the reunion."

"We'll be there, but I don't know why you want me. I hear you already got more celebrities lined up than California's got wine-tasters."

"It's shaping up to be festive."

"I know what would make it more festive for me."

"What?"

"Round up some of these imbeciles who've ruined the NFL for me. Let me have a piece of their ass. They're responsible for me joining Donna Lou in the den on Sundays to watch house flippers or fat girls try on wedding gowns."

"It's the protestors you speak of, I'm guessing."

"Protestors, huh? If that's how you want to dignify 'em. I've said from the start that any sumbitch who gets rich playing a game but won't stand for our anthem . . . won't show respect for the flag and country he's lucky to be born in . . . a country that brave Americans fight and die for . . . he ought to be sent to live in a mud cave. See how he likes it. I'm not sure those kneeling turds can get me back in the audience."

"You don't think you're being a trifle harsh?"

He said, "What the hell do they have to bitch about, Tommy Earl? Oh, I forgot. Social justice. You know what *social justice* is to them? The police officer ought to stand still and let the thug shoot him first."

I said, "Billy Clyde and I laugh at 'em. They aren't smart enough to know a con job if it throws a chop-block on 'em. Some hired-help activist talks political crap to 'em, and they fall for it."

* * * * *

T. J. said, "Those jackasses make me wish I still coached. I'd remind 'em how easy they can be replaced. There are hundreds of kids playing major college football, and they'd love to take those pro jobs. Some are better players anyhow."

"I don't doubt it," I said. "All you have to do is check out the Washington Redskins from time to time."

T. J. said, "Like the old rodeo cowboy says, 'It's hard to ride 'em if you can't get 'em in the chute.'"

"See there, Coach," I said. "All that's why you'll be the reunion's star attraction, my man."

17.

ONE LAST out-of-town couple had to be nailed down before I declared victory. That was Jim Tom Pinch and his wife, the former Iris McKinney, a good old Texas gal who could pass for saucy. Jim Tom, as I've mentioned, had become a sportswriter in New York City with all of the stripes, braid, and badges that came with it.

He had spent fifteen years writing for *The Fort Worth Light & Shopper*, a newspaper born in 1922 but the first daily in this modern age to be shut down overnight. The grocery ads couldn't keep it breathing forever.

He escaped ahead of the paper's collapse. He'd sent samples of his work to the editor of *The Sports Magazine*, the power-house sports weekly, and was hired. He moved to Manhattan and in no time became one of SM's most reliable writers.

Jim Tom and Iris met and were stricken in Gully Creek when he was there to do a piece on the Tornadoes. Iris had been brought on board from her accounting job with a concrete company by her friend Kelly Sue Woodley. Iris was hired to help out in the front office when Billy Clyde was the general manager.

She and Jim Tom had lived in the common-law world for a while—Iris was against marriage.

Iris said as she had observed it, "Marriage is for people who like to argue about shit."

But she gave in one day and they made it legit.

Jim Tom was holding onto the competitive drive that living in Manhattan stirs up in people. Or so I've heard. He laughs at the stroke his national byline wields amid the agony and ecstasy of the sports world.

"If I'm not at the Super Bowl," he jokes, "they cancel it."

There are drawbacks that didn't exist in his early years at the magazine. His reliable editors were more helpful then. They handled his copy delicately when he was on deadline on the road, and his piece would come out reading like it hadn't been nibbled on by squirrels.

Today Jim Tom is forced to get along with a collection of ambitious young editors that were schooled by academics, none of whom had worked a day on a newspaper or magazine with deadlines. The academics replaced the professionals who were talked into taking early retirement or buyouts when the publication went on a cost-cutting binge.

Jim Tom referred to the new breed of editors as "the egg whites." He claims they are known to lapse into severe depression if they lose a comma war to a staff writer like, for instance, him.

There was one good friend and editor left on the staff. That was Reg Blake, a seasoned vet at the magazine. They had fun arguing politics—Reg the Red Menace, Jim Tom the Vast Right-Wing Conspiracy.

"If it gets serious," Jim Tom says, "we settle it at ping pong."

He was considering taking early retirement, becoming a contract writer, and moving somewhere easier on his whip-out. Somewhere affordable other than an Eskimo community in Siberia or a village of pygmies in Uganda.

He said, "You can't buy a broom closet in Manhattan for less than two million dollars today. Our apartment rent has ballooned to six thousand a month because there's a working fireplace in the living room."

On the side he'd written two autobiographies of sports heroes that flirted with best-sellerdom. One of course was with Billy Clyde. The other was with "Rats" Keener, the basketball coach at Kentucky who won five NCAA championships with teams on which you couldn't find a player who spoke English.

Jim Tom spent the first couple of years celebrating the fact that he'd made it to the bigtime. He'd become part of everything New York City represented. The skyscrapers, Times Square, Rockefeller Center, the Plaza Hotel, Yankee Stadium, Broadway, Sardi's, "21," P. J. Clarke's, Saks Fifth Avenue. One of the first things he did was find out where Tin Pan Alley had been. He'd seen enough movie musicals to make him curious about it.

He found out it had been a stretch of West Twenty-Eighth Street between Broadway and Sixth Avenue. But he also discovered that popular music had since then moved to the Brill Building at Forty-Ninth and Broadway.

As the magic began to wear off, Jim Tom next found himself hopping from one deadline event to another. Which brings him up to date where he's finding it harder to live comfortably in what he now calls "the Manhattan money funnel."

On the phone, he said, "Tommy Earl, when I came to New York a cab to LaGuardia was six bucks. Now it's fifteen dollars to go six blocks in Manhattan, and the guy at the wheel is an illegal from Bangladesh who not only expects me to speak Bengali, he'll have no understanding of what a red signal light means."

Then there were Iris's wishes to consider.

Iris is a likable redhead if you don't count off too many points for her mouth. If anyone could drop more four-letter words than T. J. Lambert in one conversation, it was Iris. And if anybody disliked New York City more than Big Ed Bookman, it was Iris.

The magic that Jim Tom once felt about Manhattan never gripped Iris. Her take on the Apple:

"I'm supposed to appreciate the *culture* this city offers? What culture is that? The insufferable traffic? The head-throbbing congestion? The brain-crushing noise? The outrageous cost of everything? It's a melting pot, all right."

She would tell you, "You want to make me happy? Plant my butt someplace like Sag Harbor where I can breathe fresh air, not get pushed off the sidewalk by a Center of the Universe, and be forced to stand in line for thirty goddamn minutes to be honored with a seat at a lunch counter."

Iris enjoys telling about the evening when she was verbally attacked by a white chick social worker, but one who lived in a five-million-dollar penthouse apartment on Park Avenue.

They met at a dinner party in the social worker's home. Iris and Jim Tom had been invited as a couple—the social worker was a Boston Red Sox fan. But Jim Tom was out of town on assignment, so Iris went alone, mainly to see what a Park Avenue penthouse looked like.

The thing that set off the exchange was Iris letting it be known that she was a native Texan.

The social worker said, "Oh, my. Then I must ask you how you're dealing with your 'whiteness?'"

Iris fired back with, "How do you deal with yours, honey? Do you keep it under control in your Vuitton handbag or your Gucci purse?"

Iris heard gasps as she stormed out.

Jim Tom confessed they were looking forward to the reunion. It would be a welcome break from the inconveniences of life.

18.

THE MOMENT I posted the signs—one for the dining room, one for the bar—I had no idea how many sirens it would set off. I was trying to alert the diners and cocktail crowd to the fact that Herb's would be closed to the public for a private party on the day and night of August 21.

The regulars knew about it, as did the staff, and I had bought an ad in the papers which mentioned that it was by invitation only. But that didn't keep half the population on the globe from inquiring about invitations, or maybe they were interested in something else.

People who had never dined at Herb's even once showed up and as casually as possible would ask about an invitation as they paid the lunch or dinner check. I guess if you've never known a celebrity, or breathed the same air as one . . . oh, well.

It was necessary for the early arrivals from out of town to entertain themselves for a while. They were informed that Olivia and I would be occupied. We would be settling on decorations, arranging a place to put a service bar in the dining room, and finding a spot for a mic and podium for those I would ask to speak, as in entertain us with songs, dances, and snappy patter.

I told the visitors by email that they might need maps to negotiate the roadwork taking place in the old hometown. It caused detours and traffic jams all over town. A dozen freeways were under construction going nowhere in every direction. That didn't particularly fill me with a sense of civic pride.

Bobby Downs came in the bar with Dorito Bracy and Everywhere Red Fuqua to tell me they realized they wouldn't be invited, but they offered to provide security. Hang outside in case any car-jackers or party-crashers paid a visit.

Bobby said, "Everybody knows there's gonna be people here who is rich and famous."

I said I wasn't worried about it. I was continuing to work on which locals to include and which ones to cull. I couldn't invite everybody, and I hoped I wouldn't leave out somebody who might want to get even with me by puncturing the tires on my sparkling black Lexus.

Bobby and Dorito asked on behalf of Montana Slim and Boots Dunlap if the bookmakers could buy invitations.

Bobby said, "Slim used to come here for the chicken fried steak when Herb was alive. It was usually in football season when Herb could test his brain against the six-point teasers."

Red Fuqua said, "Circus Face invented the six-point teaser."

I said, "He may have. I know it was either Circus Face or Al Capone."

Bobby said, "Herb never learned that teasers are for suckers, like the stock market."

"Both have ripped my heart out enough times," I said.

Bobby said, "Slim says only five people understand money, and they are all in New York. They can make the market do whatever they want it to do. I ask him how you get to be one of the five guys. He said you start by being a crook."

Dorito said, "Boots came here for the fried shrimp."

I said, "Boots Dunlap ate here for the fried shrimp? What? He thought Herb caught them out of the Trinity River?"

Bobby looked surprised. "There's shrimp in the Trinity River?"

I turned to Red Fuqua. "Does Circus Face want to buy an invitation?"

Red said, "Circus Face don't do public . . . only when he goes to Railhead or Angelo's for barbecue."

I said I'd seen Circus Face at Carshon's on chocolate pie day. And I'd seen him in the Paris Coffee Shop going after a slice of the egg custard.

Red Fuqua said, "I didn't know we was talkin' about deezerts."

I said the guys could tell Slim and Boots they would receive invitations in the mail. They were local celebrities, after all.

* * * * *

LOYCE EVETTS showed up with a problem. He was currently keeping up Yasmin and Renata, and asked if he could bring one of them to the reunion.

I said, "Loyce, I've lost count, but I recall a Heather and an Amber . . . an Ashly and an Angel . . . and wasn't there an Andrea and a Tina?"

He said, "You skipped Dawn and Dagmar."

"You never mentioned Dawn and Dagmar."

"They didn't last long. Skanks, is what they were. They stole rugs, lamps, plates, silverware, and blankets from the apartments when they left. Trust in this life is becoming a thing of the past, Tommy Earl."

"Which one do you feel the strongest about. Now. Today."

"Can't decide. They're both knockouts."

"I'll help you out. Which one speaks English?"

"They're Americans," he frowned. "I don't fool with foreigners anymore. Your foreigners don't bathe regular. That was a bitch of a thing to find out the hard way, if you want the truth."

"Which one is most likely to sue you for sexual harassment?"

He gave it a moment's study. "That would be Yasmin."

"Okay. Go with Renata."

"Even though she's got some tramp in her?"

"Jesus, Loyce. Is it that complicated? Are Renata and Yasmin their real names?"

Bursting into laughter, Loyce spread his arms in a gesture, and said:

"Who cares?"

* * * * *

HOYT NEWKIRK stopped in the bar to buy a round for everybody. He was celebrating. He'd met a lady, Denise Satterwhite, who helped him land a job. He planned on bringing Denise to the reunion. Everyone considered it good news that Hoyt landed a job, but their enthusiasm tapered off when they discovered he would be selling burial plots.

Hoyt is a man with a fixed smile under his Stetson and he sports a huge silver belt buckle. He's a Texan, but he's never known whether he was born in Fluvanna or Strawn. His mother could never remember either.

Moving to Fort Worth after eighteen years in New Mexico, Hoyt became fascinated with Texas history. He didn't have to tell me that no other city in the state offers a more engaging Old West history than Fort Worth.

I'd studied and read about most of it. The Chisholm Trail, other cattle drives, especially those led by Charlie Goodnight moving his longhorn herds out of the Panhandle. I'd watched longhorns corralled at the stockyards. I'd read about the Swift and Armour meat-packing plants opening here around the turn of the century—they transformed Fort Worth into a city. And before that, Fort Worth introduced the first world championship indoor rodeo.

This was a town that welcomed the occasional visits of Butch Cassidy and the Sundance Kid, the town where Miss Etta Place opened a boarding house after Butch and Sundance bit the dust in Bolivia.

In that wild and crazy era most of downtown was known as "Hell's Half Acre." There was a moment when you could have totaled up the number of sin parlors and found that the town offered its residents precisely 273 saloons, dance halls, gambling dens, and brothels as opposed to one church.

As stats go, I call that a keeper.

Hoyt's job was selling burial plots in Pioneer's Rest and Oakwood, the two oldest cemeteries in town. Samuels Avenue was making a comeback with condos and apartments replacing the old Victorian homes in the town's first well-off neighborhood. Even Pioneer's Rest cemetery on Samuels was being spruced up. Hoyt could sell me a plot close to where Major Ripley Arnold was planted.

He said I might prefer Oakwood at the south end of Grand Avenue. That's where Olivia and I could rest near two of Fort Worth's legendary cattle and oil barons, Samuel Burk Burnett and W. T. Waggoner.

Or perhaps we might be more interested to own a plot near Luke Short, the gambler and gunslinger, and "Longhair Jim" Courtright, the US Marshal. They're buried in Oakwood, not far apart.

"You know about the gunfight?" Hoyt asked.

I said, "Hoyt, everybody but a metal head knows about that gunfight. Bat Masterson, a Wild West character himself—buffalo hunter, Army scout, lawman in Dodge City, friend of Wyattt Earp, gambler—was an eyewitness. He wrote about the gunfight in a story for the *Police Gazette*. That may have been what convinced him to change his major."

Jim Tom Pinch gets a kick out of knowing that Bat Masterson would spend his last twenty years as a popular sports columnist for the *New York Morning Telegraph*.

I said, "Luke and Longhair met in the street outside the White Elephant on the afternoon of February 8 in 1887. The marshal drew first, but Luke shot first. He hit Courtright in the thumb of his gun hand, and before the marshal could switch the gun to his other hand, Luke shot him four more times to finish him off.

"If Longhair Jim had done his homework he'd have known that Luke Short was not to be messed with. Luke had spent some of his own years in Tombstone and Dodge City. It was in Tombstone that Luke had outdrawn another gunslinger, a fellow named Charlie Storms, and put him on a slab."

Hoyt said, "I hear they stage a reenactment of the Fort Worth gunfight every year in front of the White Elephant Saloon on Exchange Avenue at the stockyards. I'll go next time they do it."

I said, "The White Elephant Saloon was on Main Street downtown when their gunfight took place. Now it's out on Exchange Avenue in the stockyards area. But like I've always said, it's better to have a reenactment somewhere than not have a reenactment at all."

19.

THE NIGHT before the big affair Big Ed and Big Barb invited the out-of-towners, along with Olivia and me, for dinner at the fortress. The fortress sits on Westover Lane behind an enormous iron gate, a brick wall twelve feet high, and a moat—to keep out the illegal migrants, illegal terrorists, illegal burglars, several illegal kidnappers, rapists, and muggers, and some that are home-grown.

Versailles stands three blocks away. Edinburgh Castle is four blocks past that, and the Taj Mahal is on the street behind the Bookmans.

New money.

All of the visitors showed up. Billy Clyde and Barbara Jane, Shake and Kelly Sue, Juanita and Slick, T. J. and Donna Lou, Jim Tom and Iris, plus two close friends of the Bookmans, Dr. O. D. ("Dog") Dawkins and his wife Savannah. They drove over from Dallas.

"Dog" Dawkins played football at TCU ten or twelve years after Big Ed. They'd become friends when Dawkins was head minister at the University Christian Church. He now heads up the Greater Dallas Christian Church, which is only slightly smaller than the Cotton Bowl. The reverend is known for his stirring sermons and lectures.

Juanita and Slick were late. They'd stopped off to see Grace, the "Mama of Sickness." She was comfortable living at the Nonprofit Clear Fork Assisted Living Facility. Juanita was filled with pride to hear that Grace had discovered a new disease, "Trinity Fever."

A person could catch it by standing too close to the Clear Fork of the Trinity, which weaves through enviable neighborhoods and manicured public parks in town.

Grace reasoned that the threat of "Trinity Fever" was why the West Fork of the river had diverted its route north of Fort Worth and veered east to join the Elm Fork that rolls past the west edge of downtown Dallas.

Juanita said, "I never knew rivers had that much sense."

Grace said, "What are you saying?"

"Nothing," Juanita said. "Just thinking out loud."

Juanita told the crowd at Big Ed's, "In case you don't know, Grace is the only resident in the facility with a medical degree."

Juanita and Slick and Jim Tom and Iris had never seen the fortress. Big Ed led them on a tour before dinner, a tour that included the three-bedroom guest cottage bordering the swimming pool, which might be the only swimming pool on the planet that's shaped like a frog.

Juanita said, "Dang, Big Ed, this ain't a home. This is a *resort*."

The Bookmans' private chef prepared the food and the staff didn't let any guest go thirsty. Staffers were alert to leap out of trees, hedges, or shrubs to pour cocktails and wine when necessary.

The chef prepared two spreads for the visitors who might be craving Lone Star grub.

There was nothing fancy about the Tex-Mex, nor should there be. The cheese enchiladas were delicate and covered in the proper amount of chili gravy. The tamales were made of mild pork and fit for church ladies. All of the side dishes achieved perfection—the guacamole, refried beans, refried rice, the dishes of queso, and corn tortillas.

I congratulated Big Ed on not allowing a fajita within twenty miles of us. A fajita is not Tex-Mex. The fajita should never have been permitted to escape from its ancestral home, which is a stove in the kitchen of a dilapidated ranch in Sonora, Mexico.

Big Ed said he would offer a sizable reward to anyone who could point out the mindless soul who invented the fajita.

The barbecue spread was just as impressive as the Tex-Mex. The beef and pork were lean and tender as my heart. The meat practically fell off the ribs. I was thankful that the steep wall of the estate was keeping out the evil pepper monster, who was guilty of trying to ruin every barbecue joint in town by making the meat too peppery for humans to eat.

There was civilized ultra-lean sliced brisket and ultra-lean chopped beef or pulled pork for sandwiches. And the side dishes deserved a salute—the tame barbecue sauce, potato salad, cole slaw, pinto beans.

✵ ✵ ✵ ✵ ✵

AFTER DINNER we took comfortable chairs and sofas on the terrace facing a huge outdoor fireplace. Big Ed, T. J., and Rev. Dawkins lit up cigars. That's where Big Ed was presented the gifts, which were planned as a surprise.

Rev. Dawkins gave him a copy of his latest motivational book, *There Wasn't No Bug Spray on Noah's Ark.*

T. J. brought him an old West Texas Tornado football jersey he'd taken to have framed.

Shake Tiller gave him a game ball signed by all the New York

Giants after they won that Super Bowl.

Juanita presented him with a disc of her new album with a proper title: *When Songs Had Melodies*.

Barbara Jane made tears come to Big Ed's eyes when she opened a large package and displayed the sign her daddy had posted in 1948 at the drill site. The site where he hit his first oil well near Midland. Big Ed had named the well:

The Barbara Murphy Bookman No. 1.

Big Barb said, "My word, where did you find that?"

Barbara Jane said, "In the attic on Winton Terrace when we were moving over here. I've kept it all these years."

Big Barb said to her daughter, "That would have been in '78. I do remember how you managed to enter Paschal instead of Arlington Heights or Country Day after we moved."

Barbara Jane said, "I cried and made Daddy call the Superintendent of Schools, Mister Graves. Mister Graves let me transfer to Paschal. I didn't want to leave the friends I'd gone to school with at Lily B. Clayton and McLean Junior High."

She nodded at Billy Clyde and Shake.

"These two in particular," she said.

Billy Clyde said, "What I remember is the transportation you got out of the deal. The silver Corvette."

Shake said, "She wasn't embarrassed about it either."

Barbara Jane shrugged. "You guys would have been happier if I'd asked for a Dodge Dart?"

Billy Clyde said, "On further review, no."

Big Ed smiled at the sign, and slowly mumbled, "Man oh man, the good old Permian Basin. Scurry County, Snyder, Midland, Andrews, Monahans . . . Lamesa . . . Fort Stockton . . . Lordy, Lordy."

Jim Tom Pinch gave Big Ed an autographed first edition of *Billy Clyde Puckett Talks Football*. He wrote in it:

To Big Ed Bookman:

Here is everything Billy Clyde would have said if he'd

thought of it.

Go, Frogs! Move the chains!

Jim Tom.

For more entertainment, Barbara Jane asked me to read the list of locals who would be on hand tomorrow night. Every name was greeted with laughs, moans, or questions.

I started with Doris and Lee Steadman.

Juanita said, "Oh, my God. She'll talk my ears off."

I said, "She talked mine off the other day on the phone. They've moved to an apartment in a retirement home on a road I've never heard of."

"Doris says if she trips over one more walker, she'll set off a fire alarm and watch all the people on walkers collide and fall in a heap."

I named C. L. Corkins and his new wife Kitty.

Shake said, "The insurance guy? He has a new wife? His first wife probably got tired of hearing him break up laughing as he read the fine print on a policy."

Moving on, I mentioned Dr. Neil Forcheimer, the TCU professor, and his wife Ruthie. Billy Clyde said, "Is he still teaching political science and his version of world history in contrast to Egypt's version?"

I said, "He's still at it. If you have tenure, you're not allowed to die."

Shake said, "What I remember is Dr. Forcheimer being in favor of free health care, food, housing, transportation, tuition, and money.

"I was in his class when a student asked him where the money would come from. He said the government. When the student asked him where the government would get the money, he said, 'They have it—that's all you need to know.'"

I brought up Foster Barton and his wife Dee Dee.

Barbara Jane said, "The funeral home guy has a *wife*? Did he always?"

"Always," said Olivia. "But you only see her if you go to the same hairdresser. Or follow her to Dallas. She's an SMU grad. Her girlfriends all stayed in Dallas and married real estate developers. Her social life is in Dallas."

Onward to Old Jeemy Williams, the country DJ, and his wife Scooter.

"He's been great for my career," Juanita said. "Don't jack with him."

"He hasn't robbed us yet either," Slick said.

The next name drew laughter from Juanita. Hank Rainey, the society carpenter. "Hank has a wife named Daphne," I added.

Juanita said, "I have a fond remembrance of Hank Rainey being the most-laid guy in town.'"

I said, "He may still hold the amateur title, but if you count the pros, he's not in a class with Loyce Evetts."

"Who's that?" asked Rev. Dawkins.

"My friend Loyce Evetts. Rich guy. Keeps bimbos on the side."

Olivia said, "Another great American and wonderful human being. Loyce is bringing one of his shapely adorables to the party. Her name is Renata."

"What's Renata's last name?" Rev. Dawkins asked.

"I've seen her," I said. "Renata don't need a last name."

Billy Clyde, Shake, and T. J. laughed.

I moved into the list of new regulars.

I began with "Montana Slim" Kramer and "Boots" Dunlap. "Gentleman bookmakers," I said. "Boots is the only person I've heard of who came to Herb's for the fried shrimp."

Billy Clyde said, "I never knew Herb's served fried shrimp."

"Fresh out of the Trinity," I said with a straight face.

I followed up the bookmakers with Jeff Sagely, the food wagon guy, and his wife Margarine. "Her name used to be Real Butter, but for reasons unknown he's changed it to Margarine. I've been meaning to ask him why."

"I do hope you'll share his explanation with us," Barbara Jane said.

"Jeff will be the guy with his arm in a sling," I said. "Gunshot wound from the last time he was ripped off by the Tango gang. It happened when he was set up in the Botanic Gardens, or what Opal Parker calls 'the Mechanical Gardens.' It's across University Drive from his normal location by the river in Trinity Park."

Juanita asked, "Why doesn't he move to a different part of town?"

I said, "Jeff says it's safer where he is than anywhere else."

Slick said, "That's why I pack. No reason why the neighborhood gangs should be the only people with guns. Open borders, my ass."

I brought up Donny Chance, the house painter, and his wife Lisa Mona. Having created the BLD—breakfast, lunch, and dinner, the Bodobber—Donny was working on an afternoon snack, which, if I understand it, is made of artichokes, salami, turkey, fried egg, red peppers, and sauerkraut with mayo on rye.

He hasn't thought of a name for it yet. I've suggested he ask a proctologist.

There were Hoyt Newkirk and his lady friend Denise Satterwhite.

A new regular, I explained. Hoyt moved here from Ruidoso where he ran a resort-casino for the Apache descendants of Dances with Cactus. I told the friends to be alert for a bargain offer in burial plots.

I almost forgot Chester Whooten and his wife Rosalie.

I said if you see a guy wearing a Houston Astros baseball cap, that's him. He's still celebrating the first major league team in Texas to win the World Series. He had been a die-hard fan of the Texas Rangers, a team that should have won the Series in 2011. But they lost it to the St. Louis Cardinals in the most torturous way conceivable. I felt his pain. I was watching on TV.

A Ranger outfielder loafed on an easy fly ball that would have been the final out in the sixth game when they were leading the Cardinals three games to two and 7-5 on the field. That hit gave St. Louis new life to tie the game. The Cards won it in the eleventh inning, then they won the seventh game to clinch the Series.

If you listened to Chester, there was a more telling reason why the Rangers let the Series slip away. They were "choking-dogs wading around in slime pits."

Then there were the Low-Flying Ducks.

I described them as two women in their advancing years who were loyal customers. There was Gladys Hobbs, who owned a dress shop nearby, and Cora Abernathy, the co-owner of a bakery.

Gladys was happy to tell you that she "couldn't care less" about anything that didn't involve her own life or business. As for Cora, if you weren't careful she would walk you through the stages of how she made the best banana layer cake in the world.

I warned everybody that the ladies were in the Hall of Fame of time bandits, room clearers, and rally killers.

"What's a rally killer?" Hoyt Newkirk asked.

I said, "A person who changes the subject the instant a conversation turns interesting."

"Whoa, Tommy Earl!" Shake piped up. "You just gave me a title for my next book."

I said, "I did?"

Shake said, "I'm calling it, *Time Bandits, Room Clearers, and Rally Killers*. It's perfect. Thank you."

I said, "Well, as you know, I've always done what I can for the overall good of mankind."

20.

BIG ED insisted I emcee the reunion. I couldn't refuse. Who was I to ignore the request of my friend, partner, guru, and fellow accomplice in wishing incurable diseases on every store-bought socialist who wants to turn the United States into a Third World picnic area?

Everybody showed up. After the cocktail hour and the outstanding chicken fried steak dinner—Will, Opal, and Sugar came out to take a bow—I stood and tapped on the mic and opened up with an icebreaker.

It was the email I'd received that morning from Nyla Macklin in Florida. I read it to the guests word for word.

"Give the staff my best. Tell them I've met two polite gentlemen for dinner companions. I excuse their pink slacks and lime-green blazers. They don't talk about anything but golf. They love to recall the day they saw Arnold Palmer up close in the flesh at a tournament in Ponte Vedra. The pink blazer said he actually touched Palmer on the arm. I have opened a gift shop and realized that people love hurricane souvenirs. They like plates and little boxes made out of roof shingles, and they like crooked tree limbs as art objects. Both were recently provided by Hurricane Claudia. I hope your visitors don't catch something that itches from the stray-dog regulars who are there tonight. Otherwise have a fun evening. Nyla."

That put everyone in a jovial mood.

I called on Billy Clyde to be the first up.

He refused to give a speech, but he had agreed to a Q-and-A session.

I said, "Billy Clyde, what was your favorite play with the Giants?"

He said, "Same as at TCU. 'Student Body Right,' they called it in college. But when I was with the Giants, it was more or less known as, 'Somebody Get a Piece of Somebody for Billy Clyde.' They'd bring everybody to block and I'd deliver the mail."

"I know you liked whipping the Jets in the Super Bowl, but what other teams did you take pride in beating?"

He said, "The Packers and Cowboys. They'd been dominating the league. It was satisfying to knock off a few layers of that 'Run to Daylight' and 'America's Team' bullshit. They were great for the league, don't get me wrong. Fans love a dynasty. But fans also love to see a dynasty crash and burn."

"Any other pleasures?"

"Giving the Giants their first NFL championship since 1956. That was a great team in '56. Gifford, Conerly, Rote, the others. Their head coach was Jim Lee Howell. Only the most avid fans will remember that their offensive coordinator was Vince Lombardi, and the defensive coordinator was Tom Landry."

"Where'd you celebrate the Super Bowl in LA?"

"Some of us went to Chasen's and stuffed ourselves on steak and chili. Later, we terrorized the Polo Lounge. When we got back home, me and Shake and Barbara Jane and T. J. terrorized '21' and Clarke's and wrapped it up at Elaine's."

I said, "What's the downside to becoming a gridiron hero?"

"Answering questions like these."

I said, "But your worshippers enjoy it. What's the worst

thing about taking a big lick from a tackler?"

"It hurts," Billy Clyde said.

"Anything else you disliked?"

"Winding up on the bottom of the pile."

"Why? Aside from getting stopped for no gain?"

"It stinks down there, Tommy Earl. You should remember that. You were down there often enough."

"Ruling out Barbara Jane and Shake, what's your fondest memory of high school?"

"Lurlene Keith."

"Oh, please!"

That rise came from Barbara Jane.

"Lurlene Keith was fun," Billy Clyde said.

Barbara Jane snapped back. "Lurlene Keith was an airhead!"

"That was part of her charm, yes."

I said, "One more question. What was the most difficult thing about your high school days?"

He gave it a thought, and said, "I'd say it was trying to learn how to do the Bump and the Hustle."

Billy Clyde acknowledged the laughter and went to the booth to join Barbara Jane and the Bookmans.

21.

IT MADE sense to follow up with Shake Tiller. He was every bit of an All-America and All-Pro as Billy Clyde. Which is how I introduced him.

Shake said, "Thank you Tommy Earl for reminding me and these people of my greatness. But you left out something important. I was more responsible for Billy Clyde's success as a running back than anybody."

"I knew I'd forget something," I said.

Shake said, "With me in the lineup Billy Clyde was left with fewer people to tackle him when he carried the ball. When our quarterback called one of my routes, a Post, a Streak, a Middle, I'd take the other team's secondary with me. Sometimes a linebacker or two. Every defense was afraid if I got even one hand on the ball, it was a catch, maybe six points."

"You're saying the defense was preoccupied with you?"

"Yes I am. When I would get Billy Clyde past the line of scrimmage, he was free to rock and roll like you've never seen."

From the booth, Billy Clyde hollered at Shake, "And all this time I thought you were running for your life."

"That, too," Shake grinned.

"Talk a little about your time in Europe."

"There are only a couple of things to say about it. I got off drugs and became a book author."

"Perhaps a bit more about that time, if you don't mind."

"I cleaned up my act when I realized drugs are a commie plot against the United States. I came to my senses one day and realized the harm they were doing to me and decided to save what was left of my brain.

"While I was experimenting with drugs in the name of entertainment, I read something I'd written and it was straight out of a novel I liked. I'd plagiarized a whole page from *Tender is the Night*, the F. Scott Fitzgerald novel, thinking I'd written those words myself.

"Soon after that, I realized I'd typed the same paragraph three times in a row on a page. That was scary. I'm thankful I was able to get a grip. And while we're talking about writing, I'd like to add that the laptop computer was God's gift to writers. I switched to the laptop when I saw one. But I keep the manual typewriter for days when electricity betrays me."

"You have problems with electricity, do you?"

"It likes to play tricks on me."

"There are rumors of an affair in London."

"She was a great English lady and a wonderful human being. But I was never going to understand soccer. I know there are strikers, midfielders, defenders, and goal-keepers, so how come every goal is a total accident?"

I said, "You wrote your book in the Cotswolds. Was there any female companionship in that part of England?"

"I confess I played the lonely Yank on occasion."

"What a shocker!"

Another outburst from Barbara Jane.

Shake said, "There was only one serving wench among them."

Barbara Jane again: "What a relief."

I said, "What's the best thing you learned during your stay in Great Britain?"

"That it's cottage pie in England, made with ground beef, and it's shepherds pie in Scotland, made with ground lamb. But I was coming home eventually. A man can only take so many meat pies."

"Last question," I said. "What's your favorite high school or college memory?"

Shake said, "They're the same. Having Barb and Billy Clyde for close friends. Sometimes, you."

* * * * *

I BROUGHT up Jim Tom Pinch next, saying, "Like Billy Clyde and Barbara Jane, Jim Tom and his wife Iris are here tonight all the way from Gotham, Big Town, the Apple, Manhattan. A small island in the Atlantic."

Jim Tom said, "I want to say how lucky I was to have Billy Clyde and Shake to write about. Not just in their TCU years but on those New York Giant teams with T. J. Lambert. They were cooperative. They trusted me to know what not to write. They never had to ask if this was off the record."

"It was convenient they never had to whip your ass for something you wrote," I said.

"A writer only knows what his sources tell him. I never burned a source. I wouldn't win a Pulitzer. All I'd do was cause trouble for the guy. An athlete's drug, whiskey, or chick habit wasn't a headline to me."

"But you've dealt with troublesome heroes, right?"

"It's rare. But there'll be the coach, manager, or athlete who says he doesn't do interviews, he hates the press."

"How do you handle that person?"

Jim Tom said, "Easy. I just say, oh, that's okay, I'd rather make it up anyhow."

"That gets their attention, I imagine."

"It does."

I said, "I know you run across the angry reader who's not thrilled with something you write. How do you deal with him?"

He said, "I look forward to it. I haven't forgotten the first time it happened. This guy came up to me in a restaurant in Birmingham, Alabama. I could see he was pissed. He said in a loud voice that I had a problem with what I'd written about a golf tournament that had been held on his country club course."

"And you said . . . ?"

"I said, 'No, *you've* got the problem, I've got the typewriter.'"

I said, "You still like your job, you've said."

He said, "Hey, I'm easy to please. All I ask for is a prime parking pass at the stadium, and a hotel with twenty-four-hour room service."

* * * * *

WRAPPING up the sports part of the program, I called on T. J. Lambert.

I said, "For those of you who haven't followed football as closely as you should, I want you to know that this man right here, T. J. Lambert, meant as much to the success of the New York Giants as Billy Clyde Puckett and Marvin "Shake" Tiller. Not that anybody ever called him Marvin."

T. J. said, "They're pals, but they're real lucky they didn't have to play against me."

I asked, "Which was the most satisfying, T. J.? Was it playing the game or coaching the game?"

"I did like to pop the man luggin' the leather. And I liked turning a fat-legged rookie into a man. But I have to tell you, I can't watch the pros now. It makes me piss blood."

"Please elaborate on that for us."

"Start with the fact that the rules suck. You can't spear no-body with your hat anymore. The block in the back is a phony foul. All it does is give a zebra a chance to be on TV. *Did you see me call that block in the back, Lillian?* Nobody knows what pass interference is. I'm not sure stripping the ball ought to be legal, although I was good at it. Now they're talking about doing away with kickoffs to cut down on injuries. The average player makes four million a year, and for that the ingrate gets to take a knee when our anthem plays."

I said, "We'd like to hear more of your thoughts on that."

He said, "Like you've heard me say, Tommy Earl. There are 125 schools playing major college football. This tells you there are plenty of kids who would love to take the place of those empty-headed saps. The fans wouldn't give a hoot as long as the replacements wear the team colors. Some might be better athletes than those knuckleheads anyhow."

"And your position would be ... ?"

"Tell 'em they have two choices. The can stand up proud-ly, put their hand over their heart, and face the American flag when they hear the anthem. The flag's easy to see. It's up there on a pole.

"It might even help if they'd learned the words to the anthem somewhere growing up, but I guess that was back when teach-ers taught kids what was good about America instead of what was bad—like we're responsible for every criminal cutthroat on the streets of Caracas, Venezuela. I would tell 'em if they can't handle my demands, they no longer play football for me."

I said, "That's the T. J. Lambert I know and respect."

He said, "It's gonna take a smooth-talking dude to convince me that life is better in a mud cave than it is in the USA. I'd hope my owner would back me up on things I ask of my players, but if he didn't, it would give me a world of pleasure to tell the spineless sumbitch what he could do with my coaching job."

"Which would be . . . ?"

"Let it crawl up his ass and die."

Applause filled the room.

22.

I CALLED timeout for everyone to re-up on their adult beverages, or a cup of Will's flavorful coffee, which was known to kick-start the heart of Tyrannosarus Rex or the Frankenstein Monster, often both.

Then I asked Barbara Jane to begin, to share some show-biz tales with us.

Barbara Jane said, "I didn't spend too much time in Hollywood. I made only four features. But I was there long enough for a fat mogul to call me everything in his vocabulary, which consisted of bitch . . . slut . . . whore . . . and something that sounded a lot like the c-word."

"Did you report him?" Doris Steadman asked.

Barbara Jane giggled. "Report him? To who? Himself?"

"They shouldn't be allowed to treat women like that."

"They do unless you never want to work in that town again. Hollywood only became interested in me to begin with because I could pass for a human being in contrast to the heroin-spiked cadavers I modeled with on the runways in New York, Paris, and Milan during Fashion Week."

She took a sip of her vodka martini on the rocks.

"Fashion model," she laughed. "It requires you to slip into something no sensible person would wear and pose with your hand on your hip while a guy blows an electric fan through your hair for the photographer."

She said, "With Hollywood, the main thing to know is it's not about art. It's about money. Nobody in Hollywood knows whether a film is good unless it makes money. If *Gone with the Wind* hadn't been a huge hit it would have been written off as a 'piece of shit,' which is every studio boss's description of a film that doesn't become a blockbuster.

"In my days in Hollywood I got a glimpse of how many brain cells are missing among the moguls. Not all. But too many.

"I was summoned to this big shot's office where he asked me what kind of a role I thought I'd be suitable for. I said I didn't think I'd be any good in a car-chase film. I would hope to be in a good movie, like the old romantic comedies and adventures the studios used to make. They've been lost among robots, laser beams, and graphic effects.

"He roared laughing. 'Oh, ho, ho. You mean a good movie? The kind where everybody talks too much and nothing happens? I made a good movie once. It went right in the shitter.'"

Olivia spoke up. "He was opposed to making a 'good movie'?"

Barbara Jane nodded. "That was the same day he cut our meeting short. He had to meet Cloono at the Polo. I knew the Polo Lounge, for God's sake. I always stayed at the Beverly Hills Hotel."

I smiled at the crowd. "I imagine most of us can guess who Cloono might have been."

Barbara Jane said, "You would be right. Another time I was called to a meeting with the director and two writers of a film I was in. I met them in this sprawling suite at the Beverly Paradise Hotel. They'd been there for three days to discuss the ending. The film was about a likable guy caught up in a love triangle. It was a war flick. But the director and writers couldn't agree on whether the brave army captain should wind up with his wife back home in Dubuque, Iowa—my role—or the girlfriend in uniform on his staff in the Arabian desert.

"I was directed to play the wife as beguiling, but not too beguiling, lovable, but not that lovable, and alluring, but not that alluring. Nancy Shaffer, who plays the girlfriend, was told to play her as sexy, but not too sexy, desirable, but not that desirable, and witty, but not that witty.

"Anyone who saw the suite where the director and writers were working—and the traces of room service—would know never to invest in a movie. I was surprised to discover that it requires that many hotel suites to make a movie.

"I watched as the director and writers yelled back and forth on the ending. Beguiling wife or stunning girlfriend? Stunning girlfriend or beguiling wife? The debate ended after the director went to the john, announcing that he could *think* better sitting on the throne.

"We waited and waited longer. He emerged after thirty minutes with his nose running, and shouted, 'I've got it!'"

Barbara Jane said, "We stared at the director, anxious to hear his solution. That's when he yelled out, 'He winds up with *both*!'

"A mogul settled the issue later. He killed me in a three-car accident on a highway while I was driving to Cedar Rapids on an icy road to visit my mother."

She said, "Some of you know I'm editing a feature I've made about the Texas War for Independence. My lead is Brick Sawyer, don't swoon, ladies. He's a Texan who grew up on a ranch and played football at Texas Tech. He went to Hollywood and got lucky while he was driving a delivery truck for a laundry and dry cleaners.

"A rich lady liked his looks and called a studio boss she knew. I pulled him out of TV. He was the lead in a hit series, *In Your Face*, that private eye thing. I used the old argument that you're not a serious actor until you've been on the big screen."

"I *love* Brick Sawyer!" a female voice said. Renata.

Barbara Jane smiled. "We were on location at this ranch house in Bandera, Texas. Brick is slouched on the porch and supposedly talking on camera about his past. Him and another Texas soldier.

"Things were going well enough, but Brick suddenly stopped in the middle of the scene. He walked over to me and said he needed a little *exposition* here. He asked me to write him a scene where he reminisced about his daddy? Where the family came from, what his father was like. That kind of stuff.

"I said I'd have the scene for him tomorrow.

"I stayed up all night writing the scene. We shot it three times but every time Brick was on camera I didn't hear him say one word that I'd written. I called a break and let him know I'd spent the whole night writing him the exposition he wanted, but he hadn't spoken a word of it. Why?

"'Oh, that,' he said. 'I did it with a look.'"

A few of the guests laughed.

Barbara Jane said, "One last story. It should have been a warning at what was to come. I was privileged to be invited to a meeting with Sid Brodsky, a legend among studio bosses due to his pile of hits and the money they made. His first question was what stars today would get me to a movie theater?

"I pretended to give it some thought, and said Michelle Pfeiffer and Harrison Ford?

"'There's a hot mix,' he said.

"I said, 'They'd be great in an adventure film. Like if they were trapped in the middle of a forest fire or something.'

"The studio boss said, 'Oops, you just killed your own idea. Do you have the faintest idea of how much that fucking forest fire would cost?'"

Barbara Jane bowed to the applause and motioned for Juanita to come up and take the mic.

* * * * *

SLICK LIFTED Juanita's Martin out of the case and handed it to the "hit-making songstress," as the trades today called her.

She strapped on the Martin, picked a few strings, and said, "I'm sorry I don't have my band with me here. I named 'em Red-Eye Gravy. They like the name. They are talented musicians."

"Mention their names," said Slick.

Juanita said, "Jody Curry is on rhythm. Davey Thorpe on bass. Sonny Branch gives us a third rhythm player, and he knows his way around the Dobro. On the piano, I have Clipper Kincaid . . . and Thermo Vise is our drummer man."

A shout from the crowd. "Do you know Loretta Lynn?"

Juanita said, "We've met, but I can't say I know her."

"Reba McEntire?" somebody else asked.

"I love Reba. She's become a friend. She's given my career a boost at every opportunity. We're talking about doing a duet album."

I said, "What male country singers do you like?"

Juanita said, "Gosh, I grew up a worshipper of Willie, Waylon, Kris. Aside from those three, I've always adored Elvis. And Merle Haggard. Ray Benson and Asleep at the Wheel keep making good music. They keep Western Swing going."

A guest wondered if all the country-Western stars go by their real names?

"You'd be surprised," Juanita said. "It's not as widespread as Hollywood, but we have our share. You can go back to Hank Williams. His real name was Hiram King Williams. He was smart to change it."

Somebody said, "What others?"

Juanita said, "Well, you learn a lot of things if you hang around Tootsie's. Patsy Cline's real name was Virginia Hensley

… Faith Hill is really Audrey Perry … Shania Twain was Eileen Edwards … Randy Traywick became Randy Travis. Toby Keith was Toby Govel … I'm still Juanita Hutchins, by the way."

She continued. "We love Nashville. It reminds me of Fort Worth. It's not too big. Vanderbilt is our TCU, and the Titans are our Dallas Cowboys. Fort Worth has world-famous museums and a world-class rodeo in a world-class coliseum and the stockyards. Nashville is world-renowned as Music City.

"We love our country ham, but you won't find the kind of chicken fried steak you know and love no matter how many of our diners you test drive."

* * * * *

"**WHAT ARE** you gonna do for us tonight?" I asked.

She said, "If y'all can hold still long enough, I'll do a medley of songs I wrote that didn't do my career too much damage."

Juanita entertained the crowd with four of her biggest hits. Each number was rewarded with generous applause.

Then she said, "Here's something I wrote especially for those of you who are here tonight. I hope you like it."

She sang:

I'm goin' back to Texas
To a favorite old retreat.
Can't wait to get there.
Make my day and night complete.
It's where my friends still gather,
And often stay too late.
They'll say don't spare the gravy
On my chicken fried steak.
There are other joints in Texas
Where you'll never be alone,

But it don't matter where life takes you,
Herb's Café is still your home.
Yeah, it don't matter where you roam,
Herb's Café is still your home.

*****

THE TIMING was incredible. Juanita finished the song only seconds before the two armed robbers in black hoodies and Halloween masks busted in the front door waving very large firearms at everybody while they shouted in a tone that was what you'd have to admit was frightening.

23.

IT WOULD not be possible to describe what happened in real time. Armed robberies are like that. You might as well try to name all the cities Jason Bourne has visited in the past twenty-four hours.

Without question an armed robbery was attempted, although it developed into a comedy of tragic proportions, or we can call it a tragicomedy, to go all English Lit about it.

I can only take you through it in slow motion from the moment when the robbers showed up until the bullets stopped flying in crazy directions.

I am able to do this now that I've spoken at length to all the guests who were there as well as the investigating detective, and studied the evidence picked up by the security cameras.

Oh, and my wound is healing.

We thought at first that it must be a joke. Why not? The robbers wore identical Halloween masks under their black hoodies. The masks curiously made them look like that goofy woman who's been running for president of the United States for most of my life.

I decided it wasn't a joke when the thug with the Mac-10

submachine gun hollered out, "We don't want to shoot nobody. We want your cash money and jewelry, is all. Lay it out on the tables for us to pick up. Most of y'all is rich. Your surrance will cover your loss. You can call this a binniss transpaction. We don't want nobody to get shot, but we'll plug somebody if we have to."

One of the robbers had ushered Will, Opal, and Sugar into the dining room.

"We don't want nothin' from you three," a hoodie said. "You ain't got nothin' anybody wants anyhow. Y'all just stand there and keep quiet."

Will said, "Can I say you fellows are making a big mistake?"

"No, you can't say that or nothin' else."

Opal said, "You thugs ain't very intelligent to be doing this."

A hoodie said, "We telligent not to be working in a bar and kitchen. That's all I know."

Sugar said, "You ain't gonna be lucky enough to work in the kitchen when you get to Huntsville, Texas. More likely you be cleaning toilets."

A hoodie said, "Y'all just shut up now. We got dealings to do with these rich people."

"Fuck you!"

That startled everybody as it came from the middle of the room.

It was from T. J. Lambert. He had decided this was a robbery, not somebody's idea of a joke.

"Who said *fuck me?*" a hoodie shouted into the crowd.

"I did," T. J. shouted back.

The robber pointed his weapon at T. J.

"You see what I'm holding here? This right here is a Hi-Point CF-380 automatic. I might have to put a bulled in your gut, you keep dancin' me around with your ass talkin' big."

Dialing up the volume, T. J. hollered back at him.

"I wonder if it shoots straighter than this Glock .40 long-slide you see me pointing at your dead-meat ass."

"You makin' me laugh, asshole. You with your little Glock."

"We'll have to see, won't we?"

I stood and butted in.

"Now hold it! Wait a damn minute! Everybody calm down. We don't want to turn this into a shooting gallery."

Now Big Ed was on his feet. "I'll take care of this, Tommy Earl."

He stared at the hoodies.

"Gentlemen, we don't need to risk an accident here. I have three thousand cash with me. I carry a roll in case a friend or an employee might require help in an emergency. You people are welcome to it. We'll make this easy. Take my money and be on your way with my best wishes."

Barbara Jane grabbed the roll from Big Ed and placed it on a table, saying, "This is my ninety-year-old father. You can pick up the money while I take him and my mom out of here and put them in their car."

"Go ahead on," a punk said. "Get the old fart out of here. But three grand don't complete our binniss. Cough it up, folks. Cash, wrist watches, rings, earrings, phones."

Out in the parking lot, Big Ed said, "What did those scamps call me?"

Barbara Jane said, "Nothing, Daddy. Get in the car."

Big Barb said, "Honey, please don't go back in there."

"Billy Clyde's in there, Mother," Barbara Jane said. "I'm certain several people have called nine-one-one when they had the chance. We'll be fine."

She hurried away to reenter the dining room through the empty bar side.

Now a hoodie was saying, "You people think we gonna settle for a lousy three thousand? Y'all think we're dumb?"

T. J. responded. "Not me. I think you're all-conference stupid . . . and you're about to be all-conference stupid *and* dead."

Staring at T. J., the thug yelled, "Man, you are wearin' me out. How 'bout I show you how this gun works?"

We watched him lapse into a struggle with the weapon. He tugged on it, his body twisting around. He couldn't figure out why the trigger didn't work. He got around to finding out the safety was on. He clicked it off and fired it, but he accidentally shot himself.

I'm not lying to anybody. He shot himself in the leg.

T. J. laughed loudly as he watched the hoodie scream in pain, drop to the floor, curl up, squirm around, and combine moaning with squealing.

We heard:

"Ah, goddamn. Ah, crap. Ah, hell. Son of a bitch. I'm shot. What happened? Fuck. Shit. Piss."

The punk with the submachine gun bent over the hoodie and said, "Dorito, you clumsy ass. You done went and shot yourself in the leg! Jesus, this ain't something we needed!"

"*Dorito*?" I said. "*Dorito Bracy*? Is that you, Dorito?"

"He ain't sayin'," the punk with the submachine gun answered.

I said, "I know that's you, Dorito. And I've got an idea who the other dirt-bag is. Bobby Downs, you miserable jerkoff?"

"You don't know who I am. I'm wearing a mask. And I ain't sayin' who I am neither!"

I said, "You're not, huh? If you know what's good for you, Bobby, you'll give up on this right now. We're willing to call it a joke, and you guys can leave here before somebody else shoots himself, or one of us."

The hoodie said, "How do you know it's me if I don't tell you?"

This was the instant when a third hoodie barged in through the front door.

He was the wheelman if things had gone smoothly. He was decked out in the same goofy-woman mask as the other two, and flashed a .44 mag.

He yelled, "What the hell is taking so long? . . . Hey, you people! Whoa! You ain't supposed to be runnin' out of here! Y'all stay put now!"

He was "Everywhere Red" Fuqua.

He didn't keep the swarms of guests from trying to sneak out the back door or squeeze through the door to the bar. Or others from turning over tables and crawling under booths to hide in case of gunfire.

The security cameras revealed that Montana Slim and Boots Dunlap were first out the back door. Bookmakers have an eye for an edge. They were followed by Old Jeemy and his wife Scooter. Behind them came Billy Clyde dragging Barbara Jane and Olivia to safety.

At the door leading into the bar the security cameras caught a skirmish involving C. L. Corkins—his wife had already fled; Jeff Sagely and Magarine, and Donny Chance with Lisa Mona. All of them attempting to push through the same door to the bar and flee the building.

With Barbara Jane and Olivia outdoors, Billy Clyde said, "I have to go back in there, see if I can help Tommy Earl. Where's Shake?"

Barbara Jane said, "I saw him shielding Kelly Sue under a table."

Olivia said, "Take this, Billy Clyde."

She handed him her Smith and Wesson .38.

Barbara Jane said to Billy Clyde, "Sweetheart, be careful. If you get yourself shot, I'll kill you!"

Now Olivia was urgently hollering into her backup smartphone to somebody at the TV station to send a camera crew over here—"and I don't mean *yesterday*, whoever you are? *Who am I?* I'm Olivia Ann Randall. I'm your damn boss!"

In the meantime. Foster Barton was escorting the Low-Flying Ducks out the back, along with his wife Dee Dee, who was flooding the place with tears.

Once outdoors, Cora Abernathy knelt to ask the Lord to forgive her for watering the lawn while her three husbands were drowning in their bathtubs.

That was while Gladys Hobbs was saying, "I couldn't care less who gets shot today, as long as it's not me."

Dr. Neil Forcheimer, the TCU professor of political science and world history, discounting Egypt, stood in the center of the dining room and delivered a lecture that the robbers may not have been in a frame of mind to hear.

"How dare you people invade my safe zone from hateful activity," the professor shouted.

The hoodies stared at him inquisitively.

Dr. Forcheimer said, "I would remind you intruders that I am protected from hate speech and activity in this establishment, as I am in areas of the TCU campus."

The hoodie said, "We don't hate nobody. We're robbers."

The professor stood his ground. He reminded them that throughout history, discounting Egypt, there were ignoramuses who couldn't control their impulses and were so thoroughly outwitted mentally they resorted to physical violence.

"Is that right?" The hoodie looked like he'd asked that in all seriousness.

Loyce Evetts, in an effort to protect Renata's perfect body, stood in front of her until a bullet whizzed past him. That encouraged him to dive under a booth.

Renata bent over him and dug out the keys to his Porsche. She scurried out the back door. It was later determined that she stole everything of value she could carry away from the apartment before she disappeared in the Porsche, which was last spotted on I-30 and moving up on Little Rock.

Doris and Lee Steadman engaged in a conversation during the danger and confusion.

Doris said, "Lee, we have to get our butts out of here."

Lee said, "I agree. We can take Park Hill to Forest Park Boulevard, and go from there to Berry Street, make a right on Berry and go around the TCU campus down to Hulen, and take Hulen to ... "

Doris said, "Lee, have you lost your mind?"

Lee said, "Okay. Instead of that, we'll take South Side Boulevard back to Lancaster, go left over the bridge to Camp Bowie, and ... "

Doris snapped, "Just shut up!"

Lee said, "What did I do?"

Doris said, "Dear God, please help me out here."

Lee said, "What for?"

Billy Clyde came back in the dining room and stood next to me.

He said, "I have Olivia's .38 in my pocket."

I said, "Do you know how to use it?"

"No."

"Your dad never took you deer hunting?"

"No."

"Dove shooting?"

"No."

"Quail?"

"No."

"Tin cans?"

"No."

"Thanks for coming."

24.

IN THE NEXT moment T. J.'s wife, Donna Lou let out a shout.

She screamed, "I've had enough of this crap!"

With that, she pulled out her own weapon, a Beretta Compact, and put a round in Red Fuqua's shoulder. The shot caused him to drop his .44 mag, topple over, cussing and clutching at himself as he went to the floor in a muttering heap.

T. J. Lambert didn't move. His long-slide was still aimed at the hoodie with the submachine gun.

Slick Henderson didn't budge either. He had already shoved Juanita onto the floor under the table and whipped out his Walther and pointed it at the same punk.

My Glock .19 was in my hand and ready to go.

I hollered, "Bobby Downs, I know that's you. I'm betting you don't know how to use that weapon. This is not a movie where somebody fires an AK-47 with no kick to it. Put that thing down. I guarantee you nine-one-one's been called. You guys are in deep shit."

The punk's voice said, "Aw, hell, Tommy Earl. You and me know them lazy cops won't be here for twenty minutes. Gimme some money or I guarantee you I'll pull this trigger and who I hit won't make a shit to me. I ain't joking. I'll shoot somebody if I have to. And I still ain't sayin' who I am neither."

"Armed robbery is a serious crime, Bobby. Give it up!"

"Tommy Earl, just gimme that gold Rolex on your wrist and let me have the roll in your pocket and I'll be out of here. Screw Dorito and Red. They always been about half-ignert anyhow."

A new voice said, "Let me handle this hunk of wasted flesh."

It was Hoyt Newkirk. He stood beside me, pointing a Colt .357 mag at Bobby Downs while looking like a man who wanted a punk to make his day.

He said to me, "I'm goin' for his gun hand."

I said, "Be cool, Hoyt."

My Glock was pointed at Bobby Downs when I said, "Better put that weapon down, Bobby. I'm gonna count to three."

But Bobby pulled the trigger on the Mac-10 and it sprayed the ceiling and walls with bullets.

The recoil knocked him backwards onto the floor. He got up on his knees and looked mystified by what happened.

In self-defense, I instantly fired two shots at him, trusting my aim to hit him in the leg and shoulder. I prayed for accuracy. I didn't want to kill him.

At the exact same time Slick, Hoyt and T. J. fired shots, nicking Bobby in the hand and arm.

Billy Clyde even fired Olivia's .38. He shattered the glass on the front door and put two holes in the floor.

I tossed him a look that said, "Really?"

Caught up in the action as I was, I didn't realize until the three punks were on the floor and helpless that one of the rounds from the submachine gun had ricocheted off something and struck me in the rib cage.

I watched blood seep through my white Western shirt, but I think I passed out from nerves more than anything else.

When I came to in my room at Harris Hospital, I was informed that my first dazed words were, "What can you expect from three guys who didn't go to Paschal and lacked proper training in the home?"

Olivia was at my bedside and I was awake to find that I was not only looking at my wonderful wife but my good pals—Billy Clyde and Barbara Jane, Shake and Kelly Sue, T. J. and Donna Lou.

I heard that Big Ed and Big Barb had dropped by to check on me. So had Juanita and Slick and Jim Tom and Iris.

Barbara Jane said, "Daddy played potentate and held a news conference. He described to everyone how you were the hero of the deal."

I said, "Did he mention how we're doing on that new hole we've dug at Comanche Stretch?"

Billy Clyde said, "He's certain you're about to zip-a-dee-do-dah again."

I smiled. "Great. A man can always make room for another Christmas tree in his field."

Barbara Jane said, "Tommy Earl, that stray bullet missed your heart by inches. I call that a bigger win than hitting another oil well. Anyhow, I have it on good authority that you can't take oil wells with you when you go off on the last great adventure. Sorry, but that's how the Skipper designed it."

Olivia smiled at me. "You were so lucky, honey. Me, too. I could have lost you for good."

Shake Tiller grinned. "I hope the other team appreciates how you held the score down."

I forced a grin.

T. J. said, "I'll be spreading it around everywhere that you took a bullet for me, good buddy."

"That version suits me," I said.

I was assured that the three clumsiest armed robbers in history would recover from their wounds and be healthy enough to serve time.

It was comforting to know I hadn't killed anybody.

Chuck Mercer, the lead detective on the case, said Bobby Downs had confessed that the heist was Dorito Bracy's idea. Dorito confessed that it was Everywhere Red's idea. Red Fuqua confessed it was Bobby's idea.

The detective couldn't help laughing when he let me in on a question Bobby Downs asked him. Bobby wanted to know if there was a chance he could be sent to a penitentiary where "they play softball at recess."

Detective Mercer left as he said, "You did good, Tommy Earl."

Olivia sat by my hospital bed and said, "You were still woozy when you first talked to the detective. I laughed at what you said when he asked you what it felt like to shoot Bobby Downs."

"What did I say?"

"You said it was the dream of a lifetime."

I said, "Olivia, I'm no good at being noble, but it doesn't take much to see that the problems of two little people don't amount to a chicken fried steak in this crazy world. . . . Here's looking at you, kid."

She said, "But what about us, Rick? I mean, Tommy Earl."

Propped up in the hospital bed, I gently pulled her close to me for a hug and kiss, and said:

"We'll always have Herb's Café."

Afterword

"The sound was born on a summer night at the old Crystal Springs Pavilion in Fort Worth, Texas, when Bob Wills and his string band were entertaining the cowboys and their ladies from 9 til Fist Fight."

— DAN JENKINS, *Baja Oklahoma*

Our father's writing had the effortless vault and jauntiness of the music he loved: classic Texas swing. It's interesting to note that Dan Jenkins wrote every bit as well about music as he did about sports. As you read him, notice the tunefulness that slipped into his prose, the tapped beat from his keyboard that imbued all of his stories and his books. His was an authentic sound, like the songs he admired from Willie Nelson, sharp and astringent and beautifully crafted, and unmistakably Texan.

Listen to the rhythm in this account in *Sports Illustrated* of perhaps the greatest college football game ever played, the 1971 meeting between Nebraska and Oklahoma:

In the land of the pickup truck and cream gravy for breakfast, down where the wind can blow through the walls of a diner and into the grieving lyrics of a country song on a jukebox—down there in dirt-kicking territory they played a football game on Thanksgiving Day that was mainly for the quarterbacks on the field and for self-styled gridiron intellectuals everywhere.

Dan and June Jenkins in Hawaii ca. 1972. Family collection.

Ben Hogan and Dan in the 1950s. Courtesy *Golf Digest*.

Now, it wouldn't do to be too grandiose about him. Dad once said, "I've fought a lifelong war against pretension." I teased him, "I take you seriously, Dad. God knows somebody has to." But he strove to be an important writer, and he not only became that, but I would argue one of the very best and most important writers of his generation—one whose breakthrough style helped change the direction of the river. His sports writing stripped away old pretenses and hypocrisies and uncovered the genuine people who accomplished extraordinary athletic feats. His novels, like all great satirical American literature, were piercingly observant and made people laugh helplessly at themselves for their own excesses.

He was a relevant voice for seven decades. The popularity of his work survived through the 1960s, 1970s, 1980s, 1990s, and well into the 2000s. He was born in 1928, had his first story published when he was still in high school, and he was still tweeting at ninety years of age.

Here is more of his music, on Jack Nicklaus suffering a devastating loss at the 1972 British Open:

He stood against one of those sand hills, one foot halfway up the rise, a gloved hand braced on his knee and his head hung downward in monumental despair. He lingered in this pose, with what seemed like all of Scotland surrounding him, with the North Sea gleaming in the background and with the quiet broken only by the awkward, silly, faraway sound of bagpipes rehearsing for the victory ceremony.

Look again, and listen, to the writing of Dan Jenkins and ask yourself if that tunefulness could have been as effortless to write as it is to read.

Dan: "Ask not what Paschal can do for you. Ask what you and your golf team and your saddle shoes can do for Pascal High." Family collection.

Dan Jenkins took writing seriously. He was a humorous writer, but a significant one engaged in a pursuit he believed was profoundly important. If his characters were often satirical, they spoke with a relentless truthfulness. The humor was his style, not his substance: He loved how great athletes could make excellence look nonchalant, and he strove for the same effect on the page. He loathed false sentiment in writing, prized candor and lightness of touch above all traits, and was a free speech absolutist. He told me, "Learn your craft. And don't ever let a piece of writing out of your hands until it's as good as you can make it." To leave potential unspent, he said, was "a kind of sin."

He didn't believe in political correctness, in couching or soft-pedaling terms, because he suspected it would lead to a broader and more dangerous orthodoxy that was the enemy of sharpness and clearly defined meaning. Here is an interesting and little-known fact about our father: he once fought a free-speech case to the steps of the Supreme Court. He had written a hilarious piece about the faded old Bon Air hotel in Augusta, Georgia, which had fallen into such disrepair it looked like a "disheveled old lady," as he put it. The Bon Air sued him and Time Inc., the parent company of *Sports Illustrated*. Rather than settle, our father proceeded from one set of courthouses to the next. He won the case in the US Court of Appeals, and the wording of a decision in his favor summed up everything Dan Jenkins believed.

The judge wrote: "Freedom of expression must have the breathing space it needs to survive, regardless of 'the truth, popularity, or social utility' of the statements."

Just after our father died, we got a wonderful note from the great Tom Watson, saying something similar. "Your dad made me think and laugh at the same time," Tom said. He added: "In this age of political correctness, we need more like him to set our common sense straight."

Dan with Jack Nicklaus and Lee Trevino, Colonial Country Club.
Courtesy Colonial Country Club, Fort Worth, Texas.

Dan and Ben Hogan in the 1970s. Courtesy *Golf Digest*.

Our father took enormous pride in becoming a successful and important writer. But he actually had a greater talent, and that was his talent for friendship. He was charm personified, and everyone wanted to know him. Actors befriended him, and so did musicians and the greatest athletes. Generally, he preferred the company of his fellow writers. But there was one new and prominent friend, however, who did manage to seduce him: President George Herbert Walker Bush—41, as he signed the letters that Dad treasured.

They shared a wit and sensibility and became friends, good enough friends that the president had our home phone number. One day the phone rang, and the housekeeper answered, and heard, "This is George Bush. Is Dan in?"

The housekeeper said, "No sir, he's run out to Popeyes for some rice and beans."

There was a pause, and the president said, "Of course he has."

On another occasion, our father and President Bush played golf at a course outside of Washington. When they finished, they joined Barbara Bush for lunch, and she began to scold them for playing at a club that didn't admit women. For the next forty-five minutes, Dan Jenkins and George Bush teasingly told Barbara Bush, "Of course it made us very uncomfortable. But we're trying to change the rules from *within* the club."

Good work and hard laughter were principles with Dan Jenkins. They were also as essential to him as breathing. Even at a sickly ninety years old he still went to his desk every day and wrote. He produced more than twenty books and hundreds of articles, and, remarkably, he managed to turn them out while lifting the family luggage, shepherding three children onto airplanes, attending school plays, paying orthodontists, and mustering college tuition. All of which he made seem effortless. His fathering style, interestingly, was not much different from his writing style: excellence disguised as ease. A foundational childhood memory my brothers and I have is the steady metal-

Dan with Ben Crenshaw, who won the Colonial Legends Award
in 2015. Courtesy Colonial Country Club, Fort Worth, Texas.

At the dedication of the Dan Jenkins Press Box at TCU in 2017.
Photo by Sharon Ellman, courtesy of the TCU Athletics Department.

lic sound of a Royal typewriter as we fell asleep, and the sound of it again in the morning. He wrote through the night.

It's a simple fact that he could have written none of it without our mother, June Burrage Jenkins, because he simply wouldn't have had the heart to. She was the beautiful and elegant collaborator who moved the pen and the keys in unseen ways. She was his most trusted reader. But most importantly she gave him the gift of a deep contentment: he never had to choose between the work that he loved and the woman that he loved. They went together absolutely hand in hand.

Dan Jenkins *loved* his life—loved it with a headlong hedonistic pleasure that was impossible to check with a doctor's advice. He loved Scotch, a lean and tender steak, a slab of crisp bacon, a fresh pack of Winstons, a new pot of coffee. His great friend Bill Brendle, a legendary PR man for CBS, summed their lifestyle up at the end of one night when they were asking for the check and thinking about how to put it on their expense accounts. Brendle told the waitress to put tomorrow's date on the tab, because, as he said, "I spent today last night."

Our father spent today last night. Yet he managed to live to ninety. How much he must have loved his life to do that. The only rightful thing to feel about that is gratitude. But we know that his readers feel something else, too. When a man like our father goes, it's outsized loss. As his friend Mike Lupica says, "It's like one hundred men have left the room." Fortunately, he left his books, with so much of himself in them.

—SALLY JENKINS,
on behalf of the Jenkins Family

Photo courtesy *Golf Digest*.